GUNMAN FROM TEXAS

Del Moffet had left Texas without a clear plan, but ten years later he is still looking for Arch Rathbone, a man who will meet trouble halfway—then chase it. From Bandera to Dodge, from Dodge to the Dakotas . . . his search was always for the man he had sworn to kill. Now, on a sun-scorched piece of Wyoming Territory, they finally stood face to face, man against man, the odds all even. Until the land slowly filled with hired guns. And suddenly the odds had changed . . . to a hundred to one.

Todhunter Ballard was born in Cleveland, Ohio. He was graduated with a Bachelor's degree from Wilmington College in Ohio, having majored in mechanical engineering. His early years were spent working as an engineer before he began writing fiction for the magazine market. As W. T. Ballard he was one of the regular contributors to *Black Mask Magazine* along with Dashiell Hammett and Erle Stanley Gardner. Although Ballard published his first Western story in *Cowboy Stories* in 1936, the same year he married Phoebe Dwiggins, it wasn't until *Two-Edged Vengeance* (1951) that he produced his first Western novel. Ballard later claimed that Phoebe, following their marriage, had co-written most of his fiction with him, and perhaps this explains, in part, his memorable female characters. Ballard's Golden Age as a Western author came in the 1950s and extended to the early 1970s. *Incident at Sun Mountain* (1952), *West of Quarantine* (1953), and *High Iron* (1953) are among his finest early historical titles, published by Houghton Mifflin. After numerous traditional Westerns for various publishers, Ballard returned to the historical novel in *Gold in California!* (1965) which earned him a Golden Spur Award from the Western Writers of America. It is a story set during the Gold Rush era of the 'Forty-Niners. However, an even more panoramic view of that same era is to be found in Ballard's *magnum opus*, *The Californian* (1971), with its contrasts between the *Californios* and the emigrant gold-seekers, and the building of a freight line to compete with Wells Fargo. It was in his historical fiction that Ballard made full use of his background in engineering combined with exhaustive historical research. However, these novels are also character-driven, gripping a reader from first page to last with their inherent drama and the spirit of adventure so true of those times.

GUNMAN FROM TEXAS

Todhunter Ballard

GUNSMOKE

This hardback edition 2004
by BBC Audiobooks Ltd
by arrangement with
Golden West Literary Agency

ISBN 0 7540 8258 X

British Library Cataloguing in Publication Data available.

Printed and bound in Great Britain by
Antony Rowe Ltd., Chippenham, Wiltshire

Chapter One

The suns of a thousand trail days had darkened his skin to a shade which made his cool gray eyes doubly noticeable, and had bleached his clothes to a neutral drabness beneath the layer of fine dust.

Both the bay and the sorrel pack horse were fine drawn, a little ribby from the long and constant travel. He rode slowly, being not yet able to see the end of the journey, yet he rode steadily, with a purpose.

Time, for Del Moffet, had lost its sharp clarity. Days had slipped into weeks, and weeks into months. Nearly a year ago he had started up the Western Trail from Bandera, crossing the Nations to ask his grim questions in Dodge. And without an answer he had pushed north to Ogallala on the Platte.

Here, where the trail forked, he had hesitated, finally choosing the eastern arm which extended through Nebraska to the old Rosebud Agency, then on to Fort Bufort, high in Dakota Territory.

But he had found nothing there, no trace of the man he sought. Wearily he turned back, coming again to Ogallala and turning westward as the trail wound along the river to Fort Laramie, then northward through War Bonnet on the stage road to Deadwood. At the crossing of the Cheyenne, the old trail turned again and led him toward the rising flanks of the Big Horns. And now he came down the short grade to the town which nestled beside the Crazy Woman.

As he swung the tired horses into the dust ribbon which passed as a main street, he saw merely another cow town, a collection of weathered buildings scattered at irregular angles across half a square mile of upland prairie.

He nudged the horses into the runway of the shabby

livery and stepped down, stiffly, as if his long period in the saddle had made him forget the art of easy walking.

The hostler pumped air in and out of wheezing lungs, and squinted at the horses' brands. Failing to recognize them, he said, "Looks like they come far."

"A short piece," Del Moffet said.

"Texas, huh?"

Del didn't answer. The hostler studied the walnut-stocked guns which hung against Del's lean hips, their holsters' noses tied down with looped buckskin. He wet his lips, and then he smiled, showing yellowed, broken teeth.

"Don't mind me," he said. "They call me Nosy Perkins in these parts, because they say I'm always minding someone else's business. Guess maybe it's because I ain't got much affairs of my own to take care of."

Del Moffet said, "What do they call this country, friend?"

"It's the upper reaches of the Powder," Nosy Perkins said. "Some call the valley the Crazy Woman range, after the creek." He jerked his thumb at the open rear door to indicate the swiftly running stream which twisted through its bushed course a hundred yards behind the barn.

"It's as good a name as any. The town's Cloud. Seth Cloud was the first in the country. He built his store alongside the creek and called it Cloud's Crossing. When the others came in, the town spread out and we built a bridge. So it ain't a crossing any more." He grinned at his poor joke, and got no smile in return.

Moffet pulled the saddle off the bay and rubbed the animal's sweating back carefully. "Water them in half an hour," he said. "Some hay and a double graining when they've cooled out." He passed a reassuring hand along the arched neck. "They've earned it."

"Staying a while?" Nosy Perkins asked, "Or riding through?"

"Looking for relatives," Moffat said. "Man named Rathbone. Know him?"

"Arch Rathbone?"

To Del Moffet it seemed as if the world suddenly stood still. He had asked that question a thousand times. He had searched courthouse records and brand association receipts. And here, beside the Crazy Woman, in Cloud, Wyoming

6

Territory, a barn man was at last giving him the right answer.

He schooled himself to speak calmly. "That's his name. I heard he was in these parts."

Nosy Perkins chuckled. "That's one way of putting it," he said. "Other folks, including Arch might put it differently and say that Arch *is* these parts. There ain't a bigger outfit this side of the Big Horns. 'Tain't everyone likes Arch, but there's few deny he swings about the widest loop we got in the valley."

Standing there in the afternoon heat of the barn runway, Del Moffet tried to recall his memories of Arch Rathbone, and nearly failed. The man's voice had been a hoarse roar, and his beard had been red. A mountain of a man, Del's mother had once said, but ten years had dulled the picture and made the edges indistinct. He heard the barn man say, "Your name ain't Rathbone, is it?" and shook his head.

The pretense of kinship had provided a simple justification for asking questions up and down the trail, but now that he knew where Arch Rathbone was, it could be embarrassing.

He wanted time to size up the country and the town before he moved against Rathbone. He had left Texas without a clear plan of action, and the long intervening miles had brought neither shape nor substance to the future. Now, though, he must find out how he could hurt the man most. Just killing him wouldn't do. Too quick and painless, too simple. He'd find a better way, but it would take some scouting around first.

The barn man cleared his throat. "What if some of the Lazy R ride in? What will I tell them about you?"

Del Moffet started to say, "Just don't mention me," but then he realized that Nosy Perkins couldn't keep his mouth shut, even if he tried.

"Tell them a man from Texas was asking for Arch," he said, and stepped out onto the slatted sidewalk.

A block away, a faded sign swung creaking in the afternoon breeze. He managed to decipher the single word: HOTEL.

Moffet made toward it. his stride lengthening as some of the riding stiffness worked out of his legs. The town, he judged, was not old. No settlement in this part of the country dated back much before the Indian troubles of ten years past. But wind and sun and winter freeze had left their mark on every building. Shoddy board and unsquared pole pine logs were ugly to begin with, and weathered false fronts merely emphasized the ugliness. So the town looked old, and tired, and beaten, like a woman bowed down by hard work and hopelessness before her time.

The street was nearly deserted. Two ponies, a battered two-horse rig and a work wagon drawn up before the general store provided the only signs of life until Moffet saw a woman come out of the harness shop. She gave him a thoughtful stare, then turned into the side street and headed toward an unpainted house. The dress she wore and the sway of her hips extended an invitation to any man with the price but Moffett couldn't have been less interested.

He passed one saloon, then a second and finally a third, and went into the hotel. At the end of the narrow, dark lobby, he banged the hand bell and waited before the high desk. A slattern woman with a sullen mouth and stringy reddish hair came from the dining room. Without words, she swung the ink splattered ledger and handed him a key from the wall rack.

She didn't even look at his sprawling signature. She turned and disappeared through the dining room door, as if nothing in life could bring interest to her weary eyes.

He watched her go, shrugged, and shouldered his bedroll. The stair treads rang hollowly beneath the tap of his peg heels, and then he moved along the upper hall until he found a metal marker on a door which matched the number on his key.

Like a hundred other hotel rooms he had seen, this one was a trap for hot stale air and old smells which had accumulated through the years. The cheap pine washstand supported a bowl and a pitcher with pinkish figures painted in a scroll upon its glaze.

The rag rug on the floor was frayed at the end, and torn in a dozen places by the passage of spurred heels. The bed was iron, once white enamelled, but most of the covering had long since chipped away, leaving the dark metal to show through from underneath, ugly and dirty looking. The tired springs bellied downward halfway to the floor, and the husk mattress was lumpy and uninviting, barely concealed by the short cotton blankets and the tattered spread.

The walls showed the only effort at decoration. The canvas duck which covered the boards was stained and far from clean, but to its woven surface someone had pinned a few illustrations cut from Gody's Lady's Book.

Moffet dropped his blanket roll on the bed and thrust up the weightless window in an effort to bring some fresh air into the hot room.

The beauty of the country beyond the town limits contrasted sharply with the ugliness at his back, and it shamed the collection of shanties and cabins which sheltered most of the town's population.

He looked across their sod roofs to the swell of the foothills and the higher reaches of the Big Horns in the near distance, and he saw a rich land, nicely watered, its prairie-like mountain meadows fat with grass. Along the swift creek was a sprinkling of scrub timber, and the yellow pole pine made a dark mat on the far rises of the higher hills.

Moffet felt an overpowering distaste for the stuffy room. He left it hurriedly, went downstairs and laid his key upon the high desk.

Out in the sun glare of the street again, he located the barbershop sign and headed toward it. Then, settling into the red plush elegance of the imported chair, he let the barber's snipping shears shorten the hair which had not been cut in nearly three months. Afterward, the barber's razor scraped away the three day growth of dark beard, exposing taut-skinned, hollow cheeks, a clear-cut jaw line and high cheek bones.

While he worked, the barber talked, as only barbers can. He talked of the valley, and of Arch Rathbone, and of the gathering trouble in the territory.

He said, "I ain't defending Arch. Arch is a man that will meet trouble halfway and then chase it. But this trouble didn't start with him."

He paused to wipe soap from the razor blade, and touch it to the strap. "No sir, it was the Bench people started the fight. They drew a line across the valley, and they sent word to Arch that any Lazy R rider who crossed the line would get hurt. Two rode up there, and one came back, and he was belly down across his saddle."

He finished the shave and covered Moffet's face with a

9

hot towel. "So now he's bringing in you boys from Texas and the Lord himself doesn't know where it will end."

With the steaming over, Moffet got out of the chair. The barber handed him a towel and a bar of soap, and jerked his head toward the rear door. "Out back."

Moffet went out. A can hung on an arm which extended from the building roof. The can's bottom had been punched full of holes, and it had to be filled by bucket from the pump. It was the only substitute for a bath that the town afforded.

Moffet filled the ten gallon can, stripped and stepped inside the shelter of the frayed canvas curtains. He soaped his muscular body thoroughly, then let the can sprinkle him. Chill from the well, the water felt pleasant and invigorating after the heat and the dust of the trail.

Refreshed, he toweled leisurely, put on the clean shirt he had brought from his bedroll, and went back in the barber shop to borrow a comb.

The barber stood beside Moffett, adjusting the sleeve garters on his pink shirt.

"You're one of the men Arch brought up from Texas, ain't you?"

Moffet decided that Nosy Perkins must have been up here already, talking. He said shortly, "I'm from Texas."

"How soon are the others coming?"

Del inspected the barber in the mirror. He saw brown eyes, soft and guileless as a water spaniel's, and couldn't tell whether this little round man was a partisan of Arch Rathbone's or not.

He said, "What others?"

"It's no secret," the barber said, and he pouted a little, his thick lips giving him a slightly womanish expression. "Everyone in the country knows Arch sent down the trail for gunmen."

"Except me," Moffet said, and fished two dollars out of his pocket.

The barber fondled the dollars with his soft fingers. "Nosy said you were looking for Arch."

"I am."

"Then why pretend you ain't one of the new men he sent for."

"Because," Moffet said, "I'm not. Arch Rathbone doesn't know that I'm within a thousand miles of here. Tell me,

10

who are the leaders of the Bench ranchers you were talking about?"

"Well, I—"

"You were ready enough to talk a minute ago."

The barber wet his thick lips. "I wouldn't want to hurt anybody."

"I asked you a straight question," Moffet said. "How can you hurt anybody by giving me a straight answer?"

"Well, there's some talk about a man named Drake— Tom Drake—but he's a newcomer. He's hardly been in the country a year. I'd say Karl Madden is the real leader. They listen to him when they won't listen to anyone else."

"I see. Now where would a man find this Madden?"

"His ranch is right at the north end of the valley, but I saw him and his girl going into Seth Cloud's store not ten minutes back." The barber paused, gulping. "You ain't going to kill him, are you?"

Moffet laughed suddenly. This fellow had less sense than Nosy Perkins. Then his laugh died.

He said, "No, I'm not going to kill him," and went back to the hotel to drop off the dirty shirt in his room.

Outside again, he headed toward Seth Cloud's store, a long, low building beside the bridge which spanned the creek. Of squared logs, it was as substantial a structure as the town boasted.

He came up the three log steps, crossed the narrow porch and entered. The room within smelled of ground coffee and spice and rope. He halted just inside the door, letting his sun-dazzled eyes adjust to the gloom of the place, and then he glanced about, noting the usual long counters, piled high. He had seen a hundred general stores like it, spread across the country from Dodge City north. It offered no novelty.

His full interest focused on the stocky man and the girl who stood at the rear counter, talking to the storekeeper. He came forward slowly, softly, knowing that both they and the smaller man behind the counter were conscious of his presence and pretending to ignore him.

Waiting idly, he studied Madden without appearing to while the Bench rancher and the storekeeper bargained over supplies. As they finished, the man behind the counter said, "You'll have to wait on the evening stage for those shells, Karl. They bought me plumb out in the last few days. Stage should be here around six."

Madden turned then. He was a square man, with fair hair, faded blue eyes, and a flat, broad face. The blonde girl beside him was a little too round of face to be called pretty, yet strikingly attractive in a manner all her own. Her eyes met Moffet's and fell away, and a faint tide of color climbed beneath her fair skin, as she started to step past him.

"One moment please." Moffet spoke to the father, not the girl. "I'd like a word with you."

Madden stiffened, and from the corner of his eye Moffet saw the small man behind the counter go tense. This, he guessed, would be Seth Cloud, the town's founder, the man who had named the original crossing.

Madden wore a single gun, belted too high for an easy draw. He wore it, as a workman would wear a necessary tool, convenient but not too much in the way. He certainly wasn't a gunfighter, yet now his big hand strayed toward the butt.

"Yes?"

"My name's Moffet."

"We know who you are."

The tone, and the manner were cold and hostile. Moffet guessed that Nosy Perkins had been around here too, telling them all about the arrival of Rathbone's first Texas import.

"I doubt it," he said. "If I could talk to you for a few minutes alone—"

"No!" the girl said. "Don't trust him, Father. Don't trust any of them."

Madden spoke without taking his eyes from Moffet's face. "I'll handle this, Karen. You stay here with Seth Cloud." He gestured to Moffet and led the way toward the door.

On the narrow porch, the Bench rancher faced Moffet squarely.

"All right, what do you have to say to me?"

Something about Madden suggested a rock, a solid mass unmoved by tide or weather. Moffet said, "You're making the same mistake the barber made, and Nosy Perkins made. You take for granted that I'm one of the gunmen Arch Rathbone is bringing up the trail."

"Aren't you?"

Moffet shook his head. "I'm no friend of Rathbone. The

only way he brought me here was by being here himself. I've been hunting him for months."

"Hunting him?"

"He stole something like twenty thousand dollars from my family."

Madden studied Moffet, and although his expression didn't change, Moffet understood that the man did not like what he saw.

"I don't believe you," Madden said.

Moffet's temper slipped for an instant. "It's been a long time since a man called me a liar, mister."

The rancher stared at him. "If you're trying to pick a fight with me you're wasting time. I know how you hired gunmen work." He started back into the store.

"Wait."

Madden stopped.

"You're a fool," Moffet said. "I don't know much about your fight with Rathbone, but I do know Arch. If he does bring in outside guns, he really means business. You'll need all the help you can get. You'd better not turn mine down."

Madden weighed that, and frowned. "How do I know you want to fight Rathbone?"

"I just told you. He stole from my family."

"And why should you want to join us?"

"Look," Moffet said. "I came three thousand miles to find him and I'm alone. I need help too, if I'm going to fight him. I don't know you, and I don't know a thing about your private war, and I don't care. All I want is to get Rathbone and I'm willing to work with you to get him." Can you understand that?

"Uh-huh," Madden said. "We'll see."

"What does that mean?"

"Just what it sounds like. We'll see. We'll watch you, and if what you say is true, then we'll consider accepting your help. But until we know, until we're sure this isn't a trick of Rathbone's to work a man into our councils, we're not taking you on."

He pushed the store door open and stepped inside. It slapped shut behind him, leaving Del Moffet alone.

Chapter Two

The Big Horn Saloon, larger than its competitors, made a certain effort at grandeur. Its back-bar was a cast-off from Alder Gulch, and its three poker tables had seen service at Virginia City. Lew Cashmere, who ran the place, had been in both camps—and had moved out, some whispered, for his health.

A dapper man, standing about five-ten and weighing a compact one-seventy, Lew Cashmere was tending his own bar that afternoon. One customer slept at a table in the rear, while up front four others played listless poker for low stakes, sipping their beer and showing unrelieved boredom.

Such was the scene when Del Moffet flipped open the batwing doors and walked over to the bar.

Cashmere looked him over and nodded.

"Your pleasure, friend?"

"Something to cut the trail dust," Moffet told him, and Cashmere slid a half filled bottle onto the bar and added a shot glass.

"Chaser?"

Moffet shook his head. He poured his drink with a steady hand, so that the brown liquor beaded about the rim but didn't spill. He raised the shot glass in a little toasting gesture, put it to his lips and drank.

Green devils jabbed at the membranes of his throat.

"Not thirty days old," he said, picking up the unlabeled bottle and looking at it thoughtfully.

Lew Cashmere's smile was bland. "We have few complaints. Our people like their whisky raw and their pleasures mild."

"Like the game." Del Moffet turned to look at the card table.

14

Cashmere shrugged. "The game is small, or big, depending on the players. You want action, you name the stakes."

Moffet poured a second drink and shoved the bottle across the bar. "Have one yourself."

"I'm in the business of selling, friend, not drinking. I haven't tasted whisky for twelve years and I don't mean to again. You stand on this side of a bar and you see things you remember, things that curdle your taste for alcohol."

"Oh, a philosopher." There was mockery in Del Moffet's tone, but Cashmere showed no resentment.

"In a minor way," he admitted. "A man has to have certain pleasures, certain amusements. I get my entertainment in a study of human nature."

"Are you studying me?"

"I'm trying to." Cashmere turned to the back-bar and opened a box of cigars. He passed one to Moffet and lighted its mate himself. When it began burning to his satisfaction, he said, "From where I stand it isn't too hard to size you up. You're from Texas. You rode in two hours ago, and your horses had come a long way. You wear two guns tied down low and now you're waiting until Buck Weaver can come in to meet you."

"And who," Moffet said, "would Buck Weaver be?"

The saloon man rolled the cigar lovingly between his thin lips. He drew a mouthful of smoke into his lungs and let it drift out leisurely.

"Maybe you don't know. Maybe you do. Mr. Weaver is the riding boss for Arch Rathbone's Lazy R. He's a man who takes many things seriously, including his job."

"Interesting."

"A warning, friend. From what little I've had the chance to observe, you're not a man who takes great pleasure in obeying the orders of others. Arch and Buck rule this range with iron hands, and I don't believe you'll be entirely happy, riding for them."

Moffet laughed silently. "Who says I intend to ride for the Lazy R?"

Cashmere's left eyebrow peaked eloquently. "No one's said what you intend to do. I'm only dealing with facts."

"As Nosy Perkins relayed them to you?"

Cashmere blinked once. Then his smile freshened. "We have no newspaper," he said. "We hardly feel the need as long as Nosy resides among us."

15

Moffet grunted. "This town beats anything I've ever seen. A man's got no more privacy than a bull in a sales ring."

"Don't blame the town," Cashmere said. "This whole valley's sitting on a keg of powder and the fuse is lit. Naturally we watch developments as carefully as we can. It's a matter of self-protection, of knowing which way the wind's going to blow——"

He halted, his eyes lifting from Moffet to cover the door, then filming slightly as if he had dropped a protective shade over them to mask his thoughts.

Moffet did not turn. In the crystal depths of the back-bar mirror, he saw that a man had paused beyond the bat-wing doors and was staring over them at the room within.

As Moffet watched, the man put both hands on the upper edges of the doors, thrust them apart and came into the room. There was the suggestion of a panther in his walk, a graceful, on-balance something that spoke of perfect muscular coordination.

He was tall, and a high, bell-crowned hat accentuated his tallness. The hat looked new and unweathered and very neat, and so did the rest of his outfit. His dark trousers were carefully creased, and folded to tuck into his half-legged riding boots. His white shirt had the fresh stiffness which only starch can give, and the small bronzed star pinned to his pocket looked like a decoration rather than a badge of office.

He let the doors click behind him, and came across the worn floor effortlessly, so lean-hipped that his single heavy gun seemed to be hanging by faith alone. His face was lean, too, with a hint of Indian straightness in the nose and the high bone structure of the cheeks. Every sinewy line of him seemed to belie his gray hair.

A hard man, Moffet thought, and a dangerous one, but not treacherous. The marshal paused at his side and laid his black eyes on Moffet. He looked Del up and down calmly, then glanced at the saloon keeper.

Still Del did not turn. He kept on watching the marshal in the mirror, and he realized that the man knew he was watching.

He heard Cashmere say, with open hostility, "You want something, Horn?"

"I want a word with this stranger," the marshal said in a voice too small and soft to fit him.

"Have it then," Cashmere said, and for an instant there was a wicked gleam deep in his dark eyes, as if he hoped there would be quick trouble between these two.

He set a second glass beside the bottle on the bar and moved to the end of the room.

The marshal waited until Cashmere had gone beyond earshot. Then he said, "I'm Boone Horn."

"Del Moffet." Del turned and extended a hand. The marshal appeared not to see it, so Del let it drop easily to the counter and picked up the bottle.

"Drink?"

"No."

Moffet shoved the bottle away from him with elaborate care. "It was you who wanted a word, Horn, not me."

The marshal said, "I neither shake nor drink with a man I'm about to warn."

"Warn me then."

Horn's voice stiffened a little. "I've seen them mild and I've seen them tough," he said, "and I can act accordingly. I want you to understand that Arch Rathbone may run this part of the range, but he doesn't run the town of Cloud. He won't either, as long as I'm marshal."

Moffet didn't answer, and his silence seemed to irritate the older man. "You are like all of your kind," he said. "You figure that a man who talks doesn't mean much. But get this through your head. If any of your bunch from Texas has an idea you're free to pull rough stuff inside these town limits, you'd better think again. That's all. There won't be any second warning."

He pivoted on his high heel and marched out of the saloon, leaving the doors flapping behind him.

Moffet stood with his back to the bar, his elbows hooked over the raised rim, watching the doors slow down. He didn't realize that the saloon keeper had come up behind him until Cashmere said, "I don't know what you're thinking, friend, but make no mistake about Boone Horn. He doesn't like me, and I don't like him—our interests are on the opposite sides of the fence, you might say—but I'm the first to admit that he's mostly performance and little talk. If you or Arch move your war into this town you're going to have Horn against you, and personally I'd rather argue

17

with a company of the old Seventh than to argue with Horn when he's feeling ringy."

"Oh," Moffet said. "You've seen him work?"

Cashmere wiped his forehead with a corner of the white apron. "I have. Boone was in Deadwood, and he policed some of the railroad camps. He never filed any notches in his gun, but that's only because he takes no pride in killing."

"What's he doing in Cloud?"

"A man gets old," Cashmere said, "and the pressures build up. Boone isn't young any more, and I suppose he thought Cloud was a quiet place to ease up in. He didn't know the range hereabouts was going to catch fire."

"What is all this talk of a range war?"

"Look, friend, I have no opinion. I run a quiet place and as long as a man minds his own business and has money in his pocket he's welcome here. I serve the Lazy R and I serve the Bench ranchers. I don't take sides and I don't pretend to know who's at fault."

Moffet said mockingly, "Afraid to mention your ideas?"

Cashmere shrugged. "Arch Rathbone came in here first. The Sioux weren't long gone when he plodded up the trail with two thousand head of she stuff and breeding stock. I don't know where he came from. Some say Texas, some Kansas. Rathbone built his spread where Beaver Creek joins the Crazy Woman and grazed his stock up and down the valley.

"But other people followed, settling along the swell of the hills to the north. Some brought cattle with them, some didn't. But Rathbone began to complain that their increase was a lot bigger than the laws of nature allow. He said the Lazy R wasn't showing two calves for every fifty head of stock."

Moffet's grin was thin.

"So he began to hurrah them. His riders made things miserable for everyone they met. They roughed the men they found in town and insisted on cutting every herd that was gathered in the valley. One family quit, and others were getting discouraged when Karl Madden organized them. These people aren't farmers. This isn't a farming country. But they organized, and they drew a line across the valley. They promised to keep their cattle north of the line, and they warned Arch to keep his stock to the south." He paused, jerking his thumb at the bottle.

18

"Need another drink "

"Uh-huh."

The saloon man went on. "Arch Rathbone is no man to brace unless you mean business. He sent a couple of riders north of the line. No one knows what happened up there. One never did come back. The horse brought the other home, lashed belly down to the saddle. Arch gathered his crew and rode north, and the Bench people were waiting for him. The crew got cut up in that fight, although no one died. So Arch sent down the trail for help. You're the first one to answer that call."

Moffet sighed. "You're wrong," he said. "I didn't come up here to help Rathbone. I came to fight him."

Cashmere had that look in his eye, the same one Moffet had seen in Karl Madden's. They didn't believe him. They thought he was playing a game, spying for Arch Rathbone. He grinned without mirth, and shortly afterward went back to the hotel.

Chapter Three

Buck Weaver was small and wiry and tough. Even if he hadn't already been warned, Moffet could recognize the toughness in the Lazy R's little foreman.

The man stamped the length of the lobby and stopped in front of Al Chase, who had been laboring with his books. "I'm looking for a man from Texas."

Del Moffet got up from his corner chair. "Maybe I'm the man you want," he called, and let Weaver examine him in the yellow lamp light.

Weaver came across to him.

"Your name?"

"Del Moffet." As he said it he watched the riding boss carefully. The odds were against it, but Weaver might have heard of him.

Weaver hadn't though. He said, "How come you rode on ahead? Why didn't you wait to ride in with Champion?"

The question caught Moffet unprepared, and he had to mask his quick start of surprise. So Rathbone had sent for Joel Champion, one of the deadliest killers the border country had produced.

He shrugged. "I was told to come up here. That's all I know."

"Why didn't you ride on out to the ranch?"

"The barn man said someone would ride in and fetch me. I waited."

Buck Weaver finished measuring Moffet but he didn't thaw a bit. "Eaten yet?"

Moffet nodded.

"All right. See you later."

Watching through the big front window, Moffet saw him join half a dozen men on the sidewalk. Then the crew headed toward the Chinese restaurant.

Moffet went back to his chair. Outside the window, Cloud's sluggish life seemed to be moving gradually into a higher tempo. He could see nearly a dozen people scattered down the length of the street, but he paid them scant attention. His mind kept milling around his own problem.

He wished he could count on more time, but he couldn't. Long before the Bench bunch made up their minds, Arch Rathbone would come to town, and he'd have to deal with Arch alone.

As for Joel Champion . . . Well, hadn't Champion promised to shoot him on sight? Damn it, he didn't want a showdown yet.

Suddenly his full attention centered on the street. The floozy he'd noticed that afternoon had come out of a side alley, walking with a younger girl. They had started down toward the hotel, and then the marshal had stepped from one of the saloon doorways to intercept them.

They stood arguing. Finally the girls turned back, angry, outwardly defiant, yet obeying. But they didn't interest Moffet. He watched Boone Horn as the marshal moved slowly back along the far side of the thoroughfare, crossing one doorway and then another, stopping to peer into every saloon and restaurant he passed.

Moffet understood exactly what was in the marshal's mind. He too had patrolled streets like that—quiet, deceptively quiet streets—knowing that at any moment the whole town could explode, knowing that he walked alone, with the full responsibility for public order and safety pressing down on him.

He recalled something that Captain Webber of the Rangers had told him when he first joined. "A man with a star," the captain had said, "is of necessity the loneliest man in the world."

Then he saw the marshal pause and stare toward the bridge at the lower end of the street, and he shifted to see what had attracted Horn.

He heard the whisper of running horses, the clatter of wagon rims on the wooden bridge, and then a buckboard crossed the band of yellow light thrown by a saloon window.

He was surprised to see two girls in the front seat. The driver wore no hat, and her red hair streamed free in the evening breeze as she tooled the team up the broad ribbon of dust and swung them in to the rack before the hotel.

He watched the dark haired girl at her side jump down and run forward to fasten the nervous horses at the rack. Then the redhead joined her. They came up the steps together and entered the lobby, advancing toward the desk with a casual glance in his direction.

He did not turn. Behind him he heard Al Chase say, "Why, Sarah Rathbone. We didn't expect you tonight."

Moffet heard her answer, "Are we too late for supper, Al?"

"I'll have the woman get something up for you. How is it, Belle? We haven't see old Pete in some spell."

The dark haired girl's murmur was lost to Moffet's ears. He pivoted in his chair so he could watch the girls waiting at the desk, their backs toward him. He wasted no time on the slight brunette. The redhead fascinated him. He should have recognized her Rathbone coloring and stature the moment he saw it.

It came as a shock to realize that not once had he thought of Rathbone as a family man. He tried to search his memory for some chance reference to this girl, and found none.

They were moving into the dining room now, out of his sight, and he sat gripping the arms of the chair. Arch Rathbone had taught him to ride, to shoot, to rope. Arch had been his idol, the only truly happy memory of a disordered childhood, and when he had first heard that the big man

21

was a thief his heart had refused to believe it. But his mind had believed, because you believe a dying man. The dying have little reason to lie, and the certainty of belief had continued. Arch Rathbone, whom his father had trusted, was a thief.

So his anger had grown. No one likes to be a fool in his own eyes, and Moffet felt the fool, having idolized a thief. When anger became hate, it had sent him up the long trail, bent on revenge. He was in Cloud now to ruin Arch Rathbone, as Rathbone's failure of trust had ruined his family.

But to fight a man intelligently you must know his strengths, his weaknesses, everything about him. This girl just seemed to complicate the job.

He rose and went to the desk, saying in an easy voice, "That Rathbone's daughter?"

"His niece." Al Chase's tone was short. He too had heard the talk about this Texan, and he had no more love for gunmen than the rest of Cloud's citizens.

From where he stood, Moffet could see the two girls sitting at the long table in the dining room. The dark one was not only smaller than Sarah Rathbone, but more delicately made. Her face had a certain elfin quality which made her attractive without being beautiful.

She sat quietly, seeming to listen as Sarah Rathbone talked. But her large dark eyes were fixed on something across the room, and Moffet guessed that her mind had strayed.

On sudden impulse he entered the room. He walked directly to the table, pulling out a chair which faced theirs.

"Mind if I sit down?"

Both girls looked up, startled. Then Sarah Rathbone smiled, and the depth of her voice reminded him of Arch.

"This is a public dining room," she said. "You don't need our permission."

Moffet settled into the chair He glanced at the dark girl, wondering what her relationship to the Rathbones might be, but she had gone back to staring at the wall. He concentrated on Sarah Rathbone.

"The clerk tells me you're Arch Rathbone's niece," he said. "I used to know Arch, a long time ago."

He saw the gray-green eyes brighten.

"You did? In Texas, I'll bet. You sound like a Texan."

"Right," he said. "Arch used to work for my father."

22

"Oh. Then you must be one of the Moffets."

He was surprised that she knew the name. "I'm Del."

"Of course." He could not be certain but it seemed to him that she had become a little wary. "This is Belle Storm."

He bowed. The dark girl continued to ignore him as if she had not even heard Sarah's words. Sarah laughed.

"Don't mind Belle. She's shy, especially where men are concerned."

A blush coppered the girl's cheeks. She looked down at her hands, which were fumbling with the napkin in her lap.

Sarah's laugh deepened, and then she sobered as she said to Moffet, "This is a surprise. Wait until Arch finds that you are here."

Moffet started to say, "Wait until he does," but the sound of a shot interrupted him. Loud shouts rose in the street.

Sarah called, "Al, what's happening?"

Al Chase was still behind his desk, staring through the broad windows. His voice cracked with excitement.

"It's your crew. They've got Karl Madden cornered."

For an instant no one at the table moved, and in that instant Moffet understood that this was his chance, his opportunity to prove to the Bench ranchers that he would fight on their side against Arch Rathbone.

He leaped up and kicked the chair out of his way. He ran past Al Chase, covered the length of the lobby and burst out onto the porch.

Below him, the street which had been so quiet only a few minutes ago seemed to boil with men. He saw Madden rearing up in his wagon almost directly before the hotel. Two Lazy R riders stood at the horses' heads, holding them as they spooked in the noisy confusion. The others, with Buck Weaver in the vanguard, were trying to climb into the wagon.

Madden had dropped his reins and siezed the heavy whip and flailed it at his attackers. As Moffet reached the porch the big rancher seemed to realize that the whip was useless. He hurled it in Buck Weaver's face and reached for his gun.

His motion was painfully slow. He had not lifted the gun more than half way from the holster when the shot rang out. Moffet could not be sure who had fired. He saw Madden hesitate, saw the gun slip from his limp fingers, strike

23

the side of the wagon box and bound into the dust of the street.

Madden swayed, appeared to right himself and then pitched head first from the wagon.

Even as he fell, Karen Madden charged up the sidewalk from Seth Cloud's store. Her scream cut through the stillness which followed the shot. She threw herself into the dust, clutching at her father's gun.

She came up with it. Buck Weaver caught her shoulder. He swung her around, and then her long, anguished cry ran through the night.

"Help me! Someone help me!"

Del Moffet vaulted from the steps, ducked under the hitch rail and launched himself at Buck Weaver. He grabbed Weaver's coat collar and yanked the man around. He broke the grip Weaver had on the girl, and drove his fist into Weaver's jaw.

Weaver collapsed, but Moffet had no time to spare. Two Lazy R riders jumped onto his back. He spun, losing one. He drove his elbow into the second man's stomach and heard him gasp with pain as he released his hold and fell sidewise.

Someone across the wagon whipped a gun out and fired. The bullet whispered above Moffet's head and struck a post supporting the hotel porch roof. Then one of the horse holders let go and came charging in, both arms swinging.

Moffet met him halfway, taking a blow high on his right cheekbone which seemed to tear the head from his shoulders. But somehow he kept his feet, somehow he got inside the pounding arms, driving his right under the man's heart, sending his left crashing against the jaw.

He watched the man topple backward against the wagon wheel and slide down into the dust. Then he saw Karen Madden and a Lazy R rider struggling for her father's gun.

He took a step away. His knees felt watery. His head spun and one eye was closing. This couldn't go on.

He pulled both guns. He sent one shot straight up into the dark arch of the night sky. The second gun covered the two men who were still on their feet.

"Hold up," he said.

They held up, all right, and for a moment he stood there in complete control of the street, his back to Sarah

24

Rathbone's buckboard, the wagon before him, and the Lazy R crew picking themselves up slowly.

Even Karen Madden straightened, forgetting her father's gun, staring at him dully as if she did not yet quite realize what had happened.

Then the hoofs hammered on the bridge, and half a dozen horsemen swung into the street.

"Lazy R!" someone shouted. "Lazy R!"

They surrounded him. They reached down to grab the guns from his hands. He made no attempt to resist. He had not traveled northward to shoot these riders. They didn't even interest him right now. His eyes fired on the big man, sitting his huge horse, dominating the whole street. Arch Rathbone had arrived at last.

Chapter Four

Arch Rathbone stood six feet seven inches in his stocking feet, and the horse he rode had to be a special animal, to uphold both his weight and his proud boast that he could outride any man who worked for him.

He came into the street, bore down upon the group around the wagon and reined in his giant mount just before it trampled the unarmed stranger. Two of his riders swung out of saddle and grabbed the stranger's arms. Then Arch Rathbone spoke.

"Well, who are you?"

The stranger smiled up at him. Then he said in an easy, unhurried tone, "You're getting old, Arch."

Rathbone scowled. This fellow wasn't one of the Bench ranchers. How had he got into the picture?

"I never saw you before in my life," he said.

"You never saw Del Moffet?"

Rathbone swore, his voice a hoarse rumble. He reached up and pushed back his hat and ran his blunt fingers

25

through his red hair. He looked, Moffet thought, like a huge, red-brown bear.

"Del Moffet." He pulled the hat back into place, and suddenly his laugh rolled out to fill the night. "Del Moffet. By damn, you *are* Del Moffet."

Moffet had no chance to answer, for Boone chose that moment to spur up the street and enter the scene.

It occurred to Moffet that the old marshal might have delayed his appearance until Arch had brought the fight under some control, yet Horn did not hesitate. He thrust his horse through the crowd, stepped down and bent over Karl Madden's body.

After a moment Horn straightened. He put a lean hand on Karen Madden's shoulder as if to comfort her, then looked up at Arch Rathbone.

"Who did it, Arch?"

"I don't know," Rathbone said. "I just got here."

One of the mounted men snickered. The marshal did not seem to hear. He turned to Karen Madden, and his tone softened.

"What happened, Karen?"

She said slowly, deliberately, without sign of hysteria, "We came in this afternoon, Father and I. We needed supplies and we hoped to start back before dark. But a case of shells we wanted hadn't come in. It was due on the evening stage. When the stage came Father took the wagon and drove down to the office after the shells. I waited in Seth's store. We didn't expect any trouble. Then I heard a shot and ran out. I saw Buck Weaver with some of his men. They had stopped the wagon, and they were trying to climb into it. Father was fighting them off with his whip."

She drew a long, steadying breath. "Just as I got in front of the hotel Father dropped the whip and tried to pull his gun. He never got it clear. Someone shot him. He fell, and the gun fell, and without thinking I ran and picked it up. Buck Weaver grabbed me, and then this man—" she turned slightly to indicate Moffet—"came jumping off the hotel porch and knocked Buck down."

The old marshal glanced at Moffet's bloody face with no change of expression. "I wonder if you'd be kind enough to carry Karl into the hotel."

26

Moffet wiped his mouth with the heel of his thumb. "I'd like my guns back first."

"Who's got them?" Horn said.

There was a silence. Then one of the mounted men urged his horse forward, pulled Moffet's guns from his belt, and handed them over.

Del holstered the guns. Without pausing, he stooped, picked up Karl Madden and climbed the hotel steps. As he crossed the porch he noticed Sarah Rathbone and Belle Storm standing in the shadows, watching him. Also, he heard Karen Madden's heels tapping behind him. He carried the body the length of the lobby and looked questioningly at Al Chase.

"Take him back to the laundry," Chase said. "I'll have Benson come and get him."

Moffet obeyed, following Chase through the dining room and across a corner of the big kitchen. In the laundry he laid the dead man on a table and Chase brought a sheet to cover him.

He turned and met Karen's blue eyes. "Thank you," she murmured, obviously still holding herself under deep restraint.

He wanted to say something comforting but the words wouldn't come. He contented himself with a nod and went back to the porch. Again he found it in turmoil. He spotted Seth Cloud on the sidewalk and hurried down the log steps.

"What's happened now?" he asked.

Cloud sputtered with excitement. "It's Rathbone." He made the name sound like an oath. "As soon as you carried Karl into the hotel the marshal asked Rathbone who killed Madden. Rathbone just shrugged, so Horn threatened to lock Arch up. It was then Skip Fowler stepped forward. He said he'd shot Madden. He said he'd fired to save Buck Weaver's life. So Horn told him he was under arrest."

"And?"

"Arch Rathbone just laughed. He told one of his men to give Skip his horse, and he told Skip to ride out. Horn said if he tried it he'd shoot him out of the saddle, and started to pull his gun. And then Buck Weaver and another man grabbed Horn and held him while Skip took off."

The argument still raged beside the wagon. Moffet

ducked under the rail and moved against the edge of the crowd.

Townspeople who had kept well out of sight during the earlier conflict had begun to pour from the saloons and stores. At least two hundred people thronged the street, all of them watching Horn and Arch Rathbone.

"You went too far tonight," Horn was saying. "You can't do it, Arch. You can't get away with murder, even if I have to send for the sheriff."

Rathbone spoke unhurriedly, in a rumble which carried for nearly a block.

"Don't be a fool, Horn. Madden was wrong and you know it. The boys didn't want to hurt him. All they meant to do was take those cartridges. He had no call to go for his gun, and when he went for it he was asking to get shot."

Horn said bitingly, "That doesn't excuse you for taking my prisoner. I haven't lost a prisoner in twenty years, Arch."

"You lost one tonight," Rathbone said.

He deliberately turned his back on Horn, letting his eyes range across the crowd until they settled on Moffet.

"Boy, come here."

The tone was peremptory, and he had always called Del boy. Moffet could feel the crowd shift to stare at him. He sensed Seth Cloud's renewed suspicion, and knew that Boone Horn had turned to study him with bleak eyes.

He ignored them. He came out into the street and stopped in front of Arch Rathbone.

Rathbone said, "Come on, I want to talk to you," and led the way to the Big Horn.

Chapter Five

They came into the saloon together, Arch Rathbone topping Moffet's six-feet-plus by a good half head. The crowd which had rushed to see the excitement filed back into the barrooms and the Big Horn received more than its share, for everyone in Cloud was watching Rathbone and pretending not to.

Black-coated and austere, Lew Cashmere presided at one end of the bar, his almost clerical appearance marred only by the big cigar which he held clenched in the corner of his mouth.

Rathbone stopped just inside the swinging doors, surveyed the room, then turned to inspect Moffet. His meaty lips twisted into a smile that somehow failed to reach his eyes. He had large cinnamon brown eyes, but there was no softness in them.

"You look like hell," he said, his heavy voice carrying clearly above the babble of the room. "There's a wash bench out back. Use it."

He did not wait for Moffet's answer, but moved toward the rear, heading for an empty table. Del Moffet watched him for a moment, then he walked to the rear door, knowing that everyone in the room was following his progress, speculating on his connection with Rathbone.

He came out into the littered, lantern-lighted yard, poured water from the barrel into a battered pan, and with the help of a none too clean towel sponged away the blood and dust.

A piece of broken mirror had been tack-framed against the rear wall, and in its blurred surface he had his first look at his damaged face. He had not realized that so many blows had reached him.

A cut above his eye still oozed. A heavy darkish bruise

ran across his left cheekbone and his whole face felt stiff, as if the skin had been bathed in alum. The inside of his mouth was cut where it had been driven against his teeth, and his sides ached from a dozen kicks.

He went back into the saloon. He found Rathbone sitting at a table talking to Lew Cashmere. The saloon man waited until Moffet took the seat opposite the big rancher, then moved away to stand at the head of the bar. Cashmere turned his back, but Moffet realized that he could still overhear everything said at this table.

That pleased him. He wanted Cashmere to hear. He wanted the whole room to hear him brand Arch Rathbone as a thief.

Rathbone poured a drink from the bottle at his elbow and shoved the glass across to Moffet. Moffet put it down. Despite the sourness of his cut mouth he knew that the liquor was far superior to that which had been served him in the afternoon, and guessed that this must be a bottle kept for Rathbone's special use.

He set the shot glass on the table with a little thud and looked up to find Rathbone watching him. He fought down a sudden tide of warmth which built up out of memory, and saw the red beard part in a smile.

"A long time," Arch Rathbone said.

"A long time," Moffet agreed without inflection.

"I've missed you, boy. You were the only one of your breed I ever had much use for."

Moffet thought about this and realized that it probaby was true. His father had been a sickly man, made so by a Minié ball he had carried away from Gettysburg, and by the painful years he had spent in the federal prison. His mother had been sharp-tongued and weary, hating the Texas country that was so unlike her native Virginia.

He said evenly, "They're both dead. My father died six months after you failed to return from the last drive. When you didn't bring back the herd money, we lost the ranch, and we went to live with my father's brother in Austin."

"The Senator?"

"The Senator," Moffet said. "The Senator got me a job, riding for the Rafter. He said a growing boy needed occupation."

Rathbone's grin widened. "The Senator would, if it meant saving him a nickel." His snicker told Moffet that they shared a low opinion of his uncle. "So you've been riding for the Rafter?"

"I joined the Rangers four years ago, as soon as I was old enough."

Rathbone considered this. He was wary, on guard, studying this boy who had grown to be a man.

Moffet said abruptly, "Why'd you do it, Arch?" and raised his voice for Lew Cashmere to overhear.

"Why did I do what?"

"Steal the herd money."

For an instant Rathbone stared at him, unblinking, the heavy face beneath the rough beard utterly unreadable. "You're crazy, boy. I didn't take the money. When I made up my mind not to go back to Texas I gave the money to Cleaves, along with a letter to your father. Didn't Cleaves bring it home?"

Del Moffet thought, He isn't as smart as I gave him credit for being. He must realize I know something, so why is he still trying to bluff it out?

Aloud he said, "Cleaves never got back to the ranch. He was ambushed at the Red River Crossing. We got a letter from the storekeeper saying that renegade Indians killed him and stole the money. He forwarded your letter that Cleaves had been carrying."

"I didn't know that."

Moffet ignored this new lie. "My father was too sick to ride north. He sent Jarbol, and Jarbol came back to say that it was true, that Cleaves was dead and the money gone. That's when we lost the ranch."

Rathbone spread his hands. "I'm sorry about the ranch, but you can't blame me—"

"Wait," Moffet said. "Don't lie any more, Arch. Hear me out."

Rathbone waited. The only sign of any emotion was the way his big fingers tightened around the whiskey bottle, tightened until the knuckles showed white.

Moffet went on, as tonelessly as if he were making a routine report to his Ranger captain. "A year and a half ago I was sent to west Texas to investigate a shooting. The man who'd been shot was dying by the time I got there. It was Jarbol."

They watched each other, indrawn, hiding their thoughts, like two poker players each holding a pat hand.

31

"He recognized me," Moffet continued. "He told me a story to clear his conscience. He said he had lied to my father. He said that when he got to the Red River Crossing to check on Cleaves' death he found you there, and that you paid him five hundred dollars to go back to the ranch and tell the story about the Indians."

Rathbone spoke, hardly moving his bearded lips. "Jarbol always was a liar."

"That's what I told myself when I first heard him. I'd always honored you, Arch, idolized you because a kid has to have someone to look up to. But afterward I got to thinking. A dying man has no need to lie. He told the truth, Arch. I know it and you know it. You're a thief and probably Cleaves' murderer."

Rathbone said nothing.

"I thought about it," Moffet said. "I thought about my father dying, deprived of his land, and about my mother, forced to live with my uncle's family and later supporting herself with housework, with scrubbing floors. I thought about it a long time and finally I took the trail up here, looking for you."

Rathbone poured a drink with a hand that was not quite steady. "You're a fool, boy."

"Probably," Moffet said. "Most people are fools at times, but I found that I couldn't live with myself, that I had to know where you were, how you'd fared with your stolen money. I resigned from the Rangers. I started looking. The storekeeper at the Red River Crossing is dead. No one knew anything about the old murder. I went on to Dodge, and there I had better luck. I found the man who had owned the stockyard, the man who bought our trail herd. He dug through his old records, and he remembered you, Arch. You aren't an easy man to forget. He told me he bought the herd, and he told me that three months later you came back with cash and bought she stock and breeders and drove them north. I followed. It took a long time, but I'm at the end of the ride. I've found you."

Rathbone downed another drink. "And now that you've found me, what do you intend to do?"

Moffet said quietly, "To begin with I meant to kill you. But I covered a lot of miles. I camped alone a lot of nights. Killing's too easy, Arch. I want to make you suffer. I want to make you pay in part for what happened to my father, to my mother—"

Rathbone said, "I did nothing to them that they didn't do to themselves, but I doubt that you'll ever believe it."

"No."

The big man snorted. "Now you listen. I'm going to tell you what did happen. I don't know why. Maybe because you're a kid I practically raised, trying something which can't be done and will only hurt you, not anyone else."

Moffet nodded shortly.

Rathbone hesitated for a moment. "I'm not a man who's ever troubled to give an account of my actions to anyone, or tried to justify what I did. In my own mind I did what I thought was right, and to hell with it and you. It started a long time ago. Your pappy went riding off to war, fancying himself in his nice gray uniform. Quite a gentleman, your pappy, a good man for Virginia maybe, but not good enough for Texas."

Moffet did not speak.

"I stayed and ran the ranch, and I held things together, God knows how. It wasn't easy in those war years. And then the war ended and he came back and you were born. Only he was sick then and it was me who fought off the carpetbaggers and ran our brand on all the loose stock for miles around.

"I took one herd up the trail to Wichita and brought the money back—and your pappy went to New Orleans to see a doctor and lost most of it in the gambling saloons."

He paused to gauge the effect of his words, but Del didn't change expression.

Rathbone went on. "So, three years later I drove up to Dodge. Before I left your pappy offered me a partnership with him. He said I'd earned it. Sure, I'd earned it, but it wasn't what I wanted.

"I thought about it all up the trail, and the more I thought the more I knew what I did want. I'd made his ranch, and I'd held it together, but it belonged to another man. I decided to quit, to strike out for myself and build my own spread. So when I sold the herd I gave Cleaves the money and the letter, and sent him back down the trail.

"But he had hardly gone before I got a hankering for Texas. I started home myself, and when I got to the Red

I found Cleaves at the Crossing, dying. Some half-breed kids had jumped him.

"He died and I started hunting those kids. It took me nearly a month but I tracked them down, halfway to Fort Smith. I killed them and got the money back, and when I returned to the store there was Jarbol, asking questions for your father."

Moffet said coldly, "You do admit now that you stole that money."

Suddenly Arch Rathbone was angry. "I'm not one to split hairs," he said savagely. "The money I got back from those breeds was lost until I went after it, and if I'd taken it on to Texas your pappy would have lost it again. He always was bad at cards. To me it was my chance. I wanted no trouble. I gave Jarbol five hundred dollars to tell his story. I went back to Dodge and bought cattle. I came up here. There was no one in this valley except a few scattered Indians. I fought for what I have. I'll see it no other way."

Moffet kept his rising temper out of his voice. "The records in Dodge show that you sold eighteen hundred and forty-four head and that you got twelve to fifteen dollars per head. Calling it an even eighteen hundred, and an average ten, you stole eighteen thousand dollars from my family, Arch."

Rathbone squinted at him. "And I suppose you expect me to just quietly hand it over to you?"

"Giving it to me wouldn't wipe out the misery and hopelessness your taking it caused. I'm going to take it away from you, Arch. I'm going to ruin you until you haven't got one cent to rub against another."

Rathbone's laugh filled the saloon. It quieted the room and turned every head in their direction. "Boy," he said, "you've been eating raw meat somewhere and it's given you ideas. I run this valley and I wipe out those who stand against me. Remember what happened to Karl Madden tonight."

"I should think you'd be trying to forget it."

Rathbone took no notice. "And you saw what happened when that fool Boone Horn tried to arrest Skip Fowler."

Moffet said, "Horn was alone. You had a dozen men in the street."

"Horn's old," Rathbone said. "He had a name once, but a man can't live on past glory forever and he knows it.

Boone's quit and the Bench ranchers will quit. I know what you're probably planing, boy. You think because you jumped in and tried to help Karl Madden, they'll rally around you. You figure to lead them against the Lazy R. Forget it. Without Madden they'll be a bunch of sheep without a herder. They'll scatter. And another thing. I'm bringing in help from Texas. A man named Champion. Maybe you've heard of him?"

"I arrested him."

"With all the Rangers at your back." Rathbone's voice had grown mocking. "But there ain't a Ranger within a thousand miles of here. Get out, boy, while you can. I'd hate to see you hurt. I don't want to see you hurt for old times sake. I'd take you to the ranch and let you work for me, only I can't have a man who hates me. I can't have a man around I don't trust."

"You've changed," Moffet said. He said it sadly, for he was sad, as all grown men are a little sad for their lost youth, for their lost ideals.

Rathbone shook his head. "I haven't changed. I'm the same as I ever was. Only in those days I was branding mavericks for your pappy, and now I'm fighting for myself. Grow up, boy. You rode here for vengeance. Vengeance is the sorriest fare a man ever tried to feed upon. When you win you have nothing but bitter memories."

He stood up. He said, "Good-bye. We won't be seeing each other again," and strode out of the room. Men got out of his way, but Arch Rathbone did not even notice. For years, no one had dared to stand against him.

Chapter Six

Moffet sat quietly after the batwing doors had flapped shut behind Arch Rathbone, listening to the talk that swelled and eddied through the saloon. It was as if Rathbone's presence had been a dam, holding men silent, and now his departure freed all their pent-up emotions in a burst of sound.

Moffet waited. Sure enough, Lew Cashmere was moving toward him.

The saloon man slipped into the chair which Rathbone had vacated, and poured himself a small drink. He said, "The first in twelve years, but I need it tonight," and drank it neatly, almost daintily, like a woman sipping tea.

Moffet sensed that Cashmere was laboring under the heavy stress of some deep emotion, that the brittle mask he usually presented to the world had begun to crack. The way Cashmere gripped the glass, the very fact of his drinking encouraged Moffet.

"Something's happened to you," he said.

"Several things have happened since we talked this afternoon," Cashmere said. "I've seen Boone Horn defied in his own street. There's no law in the valley except the brand Rathbone makes, and it'll get worse when his Texas hands arrive."

"I thought Horn was no friend of yours."

The saloon man took a deep breath. His hand strayed toward the bottle, stopped, and came to rest on the table.

"Horn isn't a friend of mine. A man in my business is often at odds with organized authority. But I'm smart enough to know that any society needs control, and that Horn was the only law we had. Defy it once, and some of its power is gone. We could have chaos here as the result of this night's work."

Moffet wondered why Cashmere would risk talking so openly to a stranger. He said, "Why tell me? I don't wear a badge anymore."

"I heard what you said to Arch." Cashmere was coming to the point. He lowered his voice, leaning half across the table. "You hate him, don't you?" Moffet nodded, and Cashmere asked, "What are you going to do?"

Lew Cashmere was the last person in Cloud whom Moffet would choose as a confidant. He said, "Wait and see what happens, I guess," and hoped the lie sounded convincing. He had no intention of waiting. He meant to force Rathbone's hand. And maybe Cashmere could help.

"You want the Bench ranchers behind you." It was a statement, not a question.

Moffet didn't answer.

"You made a step in that direction tonight," Cashmere said. "You tried to help Karl Madden in the street. You can follow that up if you will."

Moffet watched him, not quite understanding.

"Karen Madden is alone." Cashmere wet his lips and his words gained urgency. "Alone, facing the Lazy R, facing the guns from Texas."

Moffet frowned. "What are you trying to say?"

"Go to her," Cashmere said. "Offer to take over the management of her ranch. Offer to carry on her father's fight. Promise this, if she'll stay safe in Cloud. I don't want her on the Bench until this trouble is over."

Moffet hid his surprise. "What is Karen Madden to you?"

A dull flush came up under the saloon man's skin. "That," he said evenly, "is none of your business. I'd offer to pay you, but I know your kind. You're young, and proud, and you're not fighting for money, not even for the money you say Arch stole from your family. You're fighting to prove something."

Moffet stirred.

"And I'll be honest. I wouldn't lift a finger to help any of them if Karen Madden wasn't involved."

So he's in love with Karen Madden, Moffet thought, and the knowledge amazed him. Even in raw Western towns the line between the saloon men and gamblers and "respectable" people was sharply drawn. A man like Karl Madden might patronize the Big Horn's bar and poker tables, but he would never introduce his daughter to Lew Cashmere.

He wondered if Karen knew of Cashmere's interest, but he couldn't ask. You just didn't press a man about certain things.

"I'll talk to her," he said.

Lew Cashmere warmed. For the first time, his smile seemed genuine. "Do that," he said. "Help her, and then ask me any favor you want."

Moffet rose, murmured good-bye and walked along the crowded bar, knowing that the drinkers were watching his progress in the back mirror. He came to the batwing doors and peered over them to the dark street. Most of the

37

horses which had lined the racks were gone, and he guessed that the Lazy R had ridden out.

He crossed diagonally toward the hotel and entered the lobby. Alone behind the desk, Al Chase lifted tired eyes and surveyed him without pleasure. "You still be wanting your room?"

Moffet considered him. "Have I said anything that would indicate I didn't?"

"Arch Rathbone told me you weren't staying, before he rode out."

A hot surge of anger rode up through Moffet. Rathbone was dictating to the townspeople, telling them plainly that Moffet was no friend of his, warning them indirectly to give him no aid.

But he controlled himself, saying merely, "Where'll I find Karen Madden?"

"At Benson's. It's the furniture store and undertaking place next to Cloud's store."

Moffet nodded and left the lobby. He moved down the dark sidewalk, found the doorway of Benson's store and went in.

The long front room was dark, and furniture made odd shapes and shadows in the gloom, but light showed under the door at the rear. He pushed it open and stopped. The room beyond was bare. A long low table occupied the center, and on this table rested a plain wooden box.

He knew that this box contained all that remained of Karl Madden, for beyond it, the small, motionless figure of Karen Madden sat in a straight-backed chair.

She was alone, and she did not raise her head at the slight creak of the door.

"Karen."

She looked up at him then, startled, and rose to her feet. He came forward and took her hands. He said gently, "It does no good, you sitting here."

Her blue eyes seeming enormous. "I—I had to sit a little while. It didn't seem quite fair to leave him all alone."

Moffet understood very well indeed. He had kept the death watch too, in his time.

"It was nice of you to come," she said. "No one else came, not even Mrs. Cloud. They're all afraid of Rathbone."

He felt a momentary sense of shame. He had not come

here to comfort her, or to pay his respects to the dead man whom he had barely known. He had come for his own purpose entirely.

He hesitated, tempted to lie. But the girl's simple honesty seemed to force the truth out of him.

"I came looking for a job," he said.

"A job?" Surprise stirred her faintly. "But I have no job to offer you. I couldn't afford to hire a man if I wanted to."

He said, "It requires no pay. Listen to me, Karen. I came up the trail hunting Rathbone. He stole money from my family. He practically killed them by his theft."

She listened as if she heard his voice but it had no meaning for her.

"I came to fight him," Moffet said. "I mean to strip him of everything he owns, to turn him out of the valley like a dog."

He saw her eyes flicker then, and knew that his words had finally struck home.

"I need help," he said. "I have to make the Bench ranchers believe in me. I have to get them to trust me. They will if I'm working for you, running the ranch for you."

He watched her. It was like watching a flower coming alive, a dead person awakening.

"Thank you," she said suddenly. "Thank you so much."

He frowned, a little disturbed by the effect he had produced.

"I'd quit," she said. "It all seemed so hopeless. Father was dead, the Texans coming in. But you've brought me new hope, new courage."

"You'll hire me, then? You'll let me run your place until this is finished?"

She nodded.

"You'll have to tell me where it is."

"I'll do better. I'll show you."

He shook his head. "Part of the deal was for you to stay in town."

"Deal?"

He cursed himself under his breath. He hadn't meant to bring Lew Cashmere into this.

"It's just better if you stay where you're safe. That's all."

She glanced at the crude box, then said evenly, "My father was in Cloud. You can see how safe he was. I'd sooner take my chances on the range. I haven't any friends here."

Moffet didn't know what to tell her. Curiously, in the last few minutes he had acquired a feeling of responsibility for her. He tried to fight it down, but it kept plaguing him.

"Look," he said. "If you don't go out to your place Arch Rathbone may let you alone. From what I know of him, he doesn't fight women."

"I'll still feel better at the ranch," she said.

He recognized the futility of argument. "All right. But if anything happens to me, come in and see Lew Cashmere."

That confused her. "Lew Cashmere? The man at the Big Horn? I hardly know him."

Moffet said, "At a time like this, you should be in a position to know your friends," and made his decision. "Cashmere's in love with you, Karen."

He saw denial form on her lips, but she didn't make it. Instead she said slowly, "He was a friend of Father's. Father trusted him, but I haven't spoken to the man more than half a dozen times in my life."

"Maybe so," Moffet said. "But it was Cashmere who suggested that I come to you and offer to run your ranch. The idea of your staying safe in town was his too."

"That I won't do," she said, and moved away from him. She paused at the door, looked back at the lonely box sitting in the empty room, and then led the way through the dark store to the street.

"You wait at the hotel," he told her. "I'll get horses from the livery."

"We've got to find the wagon."

"Why?"

"The cartridges are in it. The people on the Bench need them."

"Maybe the Lazy R took them."

"No. I saw them ride out. The last I saw of the wagon, Boone Horn was driving it down the street."

Moffet nodded. "You wait in the hotel. I'll see Horn." He walked with her as far as the hotel steps, then went on alone to the marshal's office.

Horn sat in the chair behind his desk. He sat listlessly,

like a man weary of life, and he showed only token interest when Moffet entered.

Moffet said, "I'm looking for the Madden wagon."

"I took it down to the livery barn."

Moffet started to turn, and stopped. He had seen the case of shells against the wall, partly screened by Horn's desk. "That's what I'm looking for."

Horn straightened in his chair. "You can't have them."

"Why not? The Maddens paid for them, didn't they?"

"You know what will happen if those shells reach the Bench ranchers?"

"I know what will happen if they don't," Moffet said. "They'll be like so many sitting ducks, waiting for Rathbone's crew to blast them out of the valley. Whose side are you on, Horn?"

The marshal stirred uncomfortably, unhappiness and indecision clear on his face. "I'm trying to stop a war, Moffet."

"By keeping one side unarmed?" Moffet snorted his disgust. "Try taking the guns from the Lazy R instead." He stepped past the desk, picked up the box of shells and hoisted it to his shoulder. He more than half expected the older man to try to stop him, but Horn didn't budge. The events of the evening seemed to have cut the heart clear out of him.

But as Moffet moved toward the door, he said, "How come you're running errands for Karen Madden?"

"I'm taking over the management of her place."

Without waiting for a response, Moffet stepped out into the nearly deserted street. He placed the box in a shadowed doorway and walked to the livery stable.

He found Nosy Perkins asleep on a bunk at the back of the barn office and routed him out. "I want my horses and a rented animal for Karen Madden to ride. I'll bring it back tomorrow and pick up the wagon."

He saw curiosity grow in the man's red-rimmed eyes. He knew Nosy would spread the news all over town tomorrow, but he didn't care.

Ten minutes later he rode down the street, lashed the the cartridges on his pack horse, and moved along to the hotel. Karen was waiting alone in the now darkened lobby, so he judged that Al Chase had gone to bed. He climbed to his room, refashioned his blanket roll and carried it back to

41

the pack animal. Then he helped Karen into her saddle and they started down the street toward the bridge, not talking, their horses' hoofs muffled in the deep dust.

Moffet rode a little ahead, and although he had been in the saddle by sunup, he did not feel tired. The fact that he had at last begun to act against Rathbone kept him keyed up, while his Ranger training made him alert to any danger that might lurk in the shadows.

He picked up the murmur of voices, even before he reached the bridge which spanned the rushing creek, and he halted, raising one hand as a signal to Karen Madden to check her horse.

She pulled up abreast of him. Far away across the tops of the distant hills, a three-quarter moon hung in the sky, giving a small radiance which turned the street darkness into a kind of silver penumbra, and in this light Karen looked at him questioningly.

"Someone's hiding under the bridge," he whispered. "They may be waiting for us."

He stepped from the saddle, drew his right hand gun and stalked ahead until he could touch the wooden rail.

Then moonlight did the rest. It showed him the man and the girl on the grassy bank beside the stream. It revealed the girl's red hair, and the man's arm about her high shoulders.

He started to back away, just as a small figure moved in the darkness beside Seth Cloud's store. His spin was pure reflex, and his gun leveled as the figure emerged into the light.

And then he recoginzed Sarah Rathbone's little dark-haired friend, Belle Storm.

"Spying, Mr. Moffet?"

He stared at her helplessly. He hadn't had a sister. There had been few little girls in his childhood, and even as an adult he couldn't claim to know any woman well. So he didn't know what to say. In fact, anything he said in the way of explanation would only make the situation worse.

Gulping, he climbed back to his horse and swung into the saddle. Then he touched the horse with his spurs and drummed across the bridge, leaving Karen Madden to follow.

Chapter Seven

The steepness of the rising grade slowed his animal so that Karen pulled to his side as they topped the crest, and they rode in silence for a mile. The trail swung west to to follow the line of the hills and then bending north, and three miles out they came to a fork which cut eastward.

Karen nodded at it. "The road to the Lazy R," she said.

"This part of the valley belongs to Arch?"

"He thinks so. For that matter he thinks the whole valley belongs to him."

"I should think you'd be afraid to use this road."

"The orders are to not get off of it."

"Whose orders?"

"Rathbone's."

Moffet twisted in his saddle to gaze out across the moon-lit scene. It was in fact a number of small valleys, each tiny stream having cut its own course out of the hills in its effort to join the Crazy Woman and be carried with those waters rushing into the Powder.

He said, "I think it's time we had a small talk."

"I've been waiting." There was a directness about her which he found disconcerting, an acceptance of things as they were that he would expect from a man.

He told her then who he was, and why he had followed Rathbone up the trail, and what he intended to do. "It's only fair that you know all about me," he said. "It's only fair that you realize I'm here for one purpose and one only—to break Arch Rathbone."

She made no comment.

"And I expect to use the Bench ranchers to help me. You have to understand that. You have to realize what my presence at your ranch can mean to you."

43

She said with deep bitterness, "My father is dead. There's nothing they can do to hurt me now."

"But you do want to see Arch Rathbone punished?"

"I want to see him dead. I'd kill him myself if I had the chance." She seemed to sense that her sudden viciousness surprised him, and she said in a slightly different tone, "I know women aren't suposed to talk that way, or think that way. But he killed my father, and my father was all I had. Don't worry, Del Moffet, you can count on me. I'll do anything I can to get Arch Rathbone."

"And how many of the other Bench ranchers can we count on?"

"Not one of them." Her voice rang with contempt. "Not one. Oh, they were ready enough to fight at first. They drew the line across the valley, and one of them—I don't know who—shot those two Lazy R riders from ambush.

"But the action scared them, and when they heard Arch was bringing in gunmen from Texas they almost ran. It was all Father could do to hold them, to make them agree to wait for the meeting at the schoolhouse tomorrow night."

He waited, letting her talk it out.

"And now that Father's dead they'll be more ready than ever to run."

He said, "What about this Tom Drake I've heard mentioned? Who is he? Will the Bench people follow him?"

She shook her head. "I don't trust him. You saw him tonight. He was the man down by the creek, with his arm around Sarah Rathbone. It's about the only way he can see her, sneaking around when Arch isn't looking. Arch would kill him if he caught them together."

Moffet digested this in silence.

"I don't even know who he is. I've heard it whispered that he used to be a gambler in Kansas. He came in here last year and bought the old Norton place. He's got a few head of cows and he keeps one rider, but Father always said he was no cattle man. Father didn't trust him."

"I see."

"Still, he does hate Arch. Arch caught him in town a couple of months ago. Buck Weaver and one other of the Lazy R riders held him under their guns and Arch whipped him with half the people in Cloud looking on. Then he gave Drake twenty-four hours to get out of the country."

"And he hasn't gone."

"You saw him tonight."

Moffet had already decided to talk to Tom Drake. Now he thought of something else. "That black-haired girl, Belle Storm, the one who was with Sarah tonight. Who is she?"

"Oh, her," Karen said. "She lives with old Pete at the fort."

"The fort?"

"Yes, it's an army post that was built fifteen years ago and then abandoned. Pete Storm took it over. He runs a kind of trading post, dealing with the trappers and breeds back in the hills. I don't like her."

"Why not?"

Karen Madden sighed impatiently, but as usual she gave an honest answer. "I don't rightly know," she said. "We used to tease her at school when we were all younger. Everyone teased her except Sarah Rathbone. Sarah always took her part, and she's stayed friendly with Sarah, even though none of the other valley women will speak to her since the trouble started."

"Speak to Sarah, you mean?"

She nodded. "Sarah's a lot like Arch. She can be as mean as he is, and just as overbearing. She treats the rest of us like dirt."

Moffet detected Karen's jealousy easily enough, and he let it pass. But all during the long ride to the foothill ranch he kept thinking about Belle Storm.

He slept in the barn, rising with the sun and stepping out into the fenced yard. Marks of Karl Madden's slow, stubborn industry were everywhere. The log house was tight, and both the barn and shed roofs in good repear. Moffet had seen too many carelessly run outfits not to appreciate the work which had gone into this place. Karl Madden had carved out this homesite the hard way, and Moffet felt that if there had been any rustling of Lazy R stock by the Bench ranchers, Karl Madden had taken no part in it.

He walked across the hard baked yard, seeing smoke rising from the kitchen chimney, and knocked on the slab door. Karen called, "Come in," and he stepped into the square room.

She stood at the stove, her cheeks flushed by the heat, her sleeves rolled up on softly rounded forearms, wisps of fair hair escaping from the tight braid which she had curled about her head.

45

She looked clean, and fresh, and by the small leap of his own pulse, Moffet understood why she had stirred Lew Cashmere out of that frozen professional calm. All through the silent meal he watched her without appearing to. He had been on the trail for months, and the hunger for a woman had grown strong.

He found himself considering. The ranch was well located, with good water, sheltered from the north and west by rising hills. A man could do far worse, and he guessed that in this time of her grief and loneliness Karen Madden would respond if he extended a hand toward her.

The possibility of marriage, of settling down, always remote in his days of trailing, seemed real now, as he ate the stack of cakes sweetened with brown sugar and drank three steaming cups of coffee.

Then, clearing the plates, Karen asked, "What do you mean to do now?"

He came to with a start. He had been dreaming as he sat idle in this tight room, with the welcome heat from the stove cutting the early morning chill, with a woman to cook his breakfast and refill his cup.

"Why, I'm going to have a talk with this Tom Drake."

"Drake? Why? I don't trust him."

Moffet shrugged. "We'll need all the help we can find if we're going to lick Arch Rathbone. I'll take the rented horse with me, and after I see Drake I'll take it on to Cloud. I may not get back here before the meeting in the schoolhouse tonight. If I don't, you take the ammunition over there."

Leaving her protesting, he went out to the corral and saddled his horse. Then, with the livery animal on a lead rope, he rode along the edge of the rise toward Drake's place.

Tom Drake's house perched on the lifting shoulder of the Bench and where Hunt Creek came out of the hills. Nearing the place, Moffet noted that the house had been built of pole pine chinked with mud, while sod sufficed for the roof. The outbuildings were mere sheds, and to Moffet's practiced eye the whole layout looked makeshift and sloppy. The corral posts leaned crookedly, the gate dangled by a rawhide thong, and litter covered the unfenced yard.

As he stepped down beside the corral, a big man came on the porch. He had never seen Tom Drake in daylight, but he knew he could have spotted the man as an ex-gambler even if Karen Madden hadn't mentioned it the night before.

Drake bore the mark. He was big, with a soft face and hard, coldly calculating blue eyes. Moffet guessed that he might well appeal to women, but the average man would distrust him on sight. And he smiled a little, thinking how angry Arch Rathbone must have been when he first learned that his niece was interested in Drake.

He came up through the yard and Drake moved off the porch to meet him, cautiously, like a big cat taking reluctant steps toward one who might be an enemy.

"I'm Moffet," he said when only half a dozen feet separated them, and judged by the flicker in Drake's eyes that Sarah Rathbone had mentioned him.

Drake studied Moffet in silence. Always he played a canny game, planning each move before he dropped a card, and here in the Powder River country the stakes called for more than the usual shrewdness.

Originally he had started northward intending to hit the rail-end towns on the new transcontinental line which was being built eastward from the coast. Just a year ago he had paused in Cloud for no other reason than to rest his horse, and then, on his first night in town, he met Sarah Rathbone.

Tom Drake had enjoyed a wide acquaintanceship among women, but never had he met one like Sarah Rathbone.

From Nosy Perkins he learned that she was Arch Rathbone's heir, and that Rathbone was as near a king as this part of the country boasted. That night, alone in his hotel room, Tom Drake took stock of himself.

He was thirty-five years old. He had begun life as a roustabout on a Mississippi river boat. Watching the gamblers in the gilded salons, he had decided that only a fool worked when a man could live as a gentleman by dealing cards.

He had learned the trade in New Orleans, and practiced it in the Western camps and in the Kansas shipping points along the extending railroads. Yet it had not brought him wealth, and unless something changed he would never gain the position of which he dreamed.

But if he stayed here, if he married this big redheaded girl, wealth and power would drop into his hands as soon

47

as Arch Rathbone died. So he made his decision that night. He would stay here.

Shrewd enough to know that Arch Rathbone would never accept a card sharp into his family, he posed as a cattle man, spending the last dollars of his sorry stake to buy a small foothill spread. But while the deception fooled Sarah, it did not impress her uncle.

Arch Rathbone had met him in town. Protected by his crew's guns, Rathbone had beaten Drake to a point where he could barely stand, and then ordered Drake out of the country.

The memory of the beating still burned in Tom Drake's consciousness like a smoking iron. After the beating he had vowed that Arch Rathbone must die, but he did not make the mistake of going after the owner of the Lazy R openly. Instead he began a careful campaign, a series of moves which would not only hand the Lazy R over to him after Arch's death, but would also empty the valley of small settlers. Thus, in the end, the entire range would come to Sarah, and through Sarah, to him.

First, Drake had incited the small ranchers to draw a line across the center of the valley. Second, using Drake's arguments, Sarah had prompted her uncle to ignore this line and send riders north. Third, Drake had arranged to have these riders killed.

Naturally, he had not appeared in any of this work. Considering Karl Madden to be the strongest, most resolute of the Bench people, he had jockied the man into a position of leadership without Madden realizing that Drake was responsible for his selection. Then he had suggested to Sarah that her uncle bring in outside help, suggesting the name of Joel Champion without mentioning the fact that Champion was an old friend of his.

He had told Sarah that once Rathbone's Texas guns frightened the small ranchers into panic, he, Drake, would buy them out. He told her further that since her uncle would never deal with him, the land must be bought in her name. Arch would hardly seize land belonging to his niece, so she could use it as a bargaining weapon, a means of pressuring Arch until he agreed to her marriage with Drake.

And Sarah believed him. She had helped in every way she could, telling him every move the Lazy R made. She did not know, of course, that Drake's plan included her uncle's death.

Yes, the stage had been set—until last night, when Sarah had told of Karl Madden's senseless murder. The news infuriated him. He cared nothing for Madden, but he knew that without a leader the Bench ranchers would not fight, and he did not want them to quit yet. And then Sarah had told him of this stranger whom she had met at the hotel, this gunman from Texas whose family had been ruined by Arch, who had ridden north hunting his former friend.

So, now, Tom Drake studied Del Moffet with great thoroughness. Given some luck, he might push this stranger into Karl Madden's spot as leader for the Bench people. He might make Moffet responsible for Arch Rathbone's death, too. For this man's personality reflected both the strength and the bitterness the role demanded.

He said easily, "I know who you are. Come in and sit down."

They sat on the edge of the porch.

"I like to lay my cards on the table," Drake began, "so everyone can see the hand I play."

Moffet laughed, a single harsh bark of derision. He had already tabbed Drake as a liar and a cheat, and the hell with pretending. He said, "I'm only interested in your hand as long as it helps me."

Drake relaxed. "All right," he said, "since we understand each other I'll be perfectly frank. There's only one thing I want out of this—to break Arch Rathbone. I love his niece. I want to marry her, and as long as Arch is the big augur around here I haven't got a chance."

"Strange way to court a girl," Moffet said, "ruining her uncle like that."

Drake's voice turned hoarse. "Do you know what he did to me? He beat me up, on the street at Cloud. He broke three ribs and my nose. He almost tore one ear off my head. If he wasn't Sarah's uncle I'd have gone after him with a gun. But I can't kill the sonofabitch and still marry the girl."

"No," Moffet agreed mildly. "You can't."

"I can ruin him, though. I can bring him to his knees and then take the girl away."

"Uh-huh," Moffet said, and sensed that Drake had more cards up his sleeve, cards bigger than a queen. He couldn't figure all of Drake's play, but he didn't need to yet. All he wanted right now was Drake's support at the ranchers' meeting tonight.

He said, "It may interest you to know that I'm now the foreman of the Madden ranch."

"Oh. I saw you riding out with Karen Madden last night and I wondered."

"And as such," Moffet continued, "I'm going to the meeting of the Bench ranchers tonight at the schoolhouse. I'm going to suggest to them that our best plan in fighting Arch Rathbone is to stay within the law as much as possible."

That puzzled Drake, and worried him a little.

"I don't quite follow," he said.

"I want," Moffet said, "to arrest Skip Fowler for Karl Madden's murder."

Drake grinned suddenly. "I'd say you might have some trouble on your hands. If I know Rathbone he'll keep Skip close to the home ranch for the next few days. Why, it would take an army to get him away from there."

"Or a posse."

"You need a law officer for that."

"What about Boone Horn? Karen Madden tells me that besides being town marshal, Horn's the deputy sheriff for this end of the country."

Drake shook his head. "You'll never get Horn to move out of town, and if you did, what would you use for a posse? There's hardly a man in Cloud who would ride against Rathbone."

"How about the Bench ranchers?"

Drake stared at Moffet, and then he began to laugh. "I like you. That would be wonderful, to have the Bench people ride legally into the Lazy R. If Arch fires on them, then he's in the spot of opposing the territorial authorities."

"Then you'll back me at the meeting?"

"I'll back you."

Drake offered his hand but somehow Moffet failed to see it. He got up and walked over to his horses. He didn't say good-bye as he swung past Drake, riding out. But Drake kept on smiling.

Chapter Eight

Wind had come up during the night, and it still blew with fitful violence, mixing a hint of cooler air with the dust and rubbish which it swirled between the unpainted buildings of Cloud's main street.

Del Moffet went directly to the livery. He returned the rented horse, arranged with Nosy Perkins to keep the Madden team until he could come again, and then swung his own horse back up along the street to the Big Horn saloon.

Lew Cashmere was alone in the long room, using a section of the bar for a desk as he went over his accounts. He glanced up idly, stiffened as he recognized Moffet, and pulled down the corners of his mouth in a show of quick anger.

"I thought you promised to leave Karen Madden safe in town?"

Moffet read the jealousy in the gambler's eyes and checked an almost overwhelming desire to laugh.

"I tried," he said, "but she refused to stay."

Obviously Cashmere didn't know whether to believe him or not. "So what are you doing back here?" Cashmere demanded.

"Lew," Moffet said, "I didn't agree to take orders from you. I'll have to handle things my own way."

Cashmere controlled himself with visible effort. "I know that. But don't you realize that your being at the Madden ranch doubles the danger to Karen?"

"You sent me there yourself."

"I'm regretting it."

"Regret it or not, that's how it is," Moffet told him. "I came to ask you a question. You sounded impressed by Boone Horn yesterday. Do you think, if I offered to raise a posse, he'd go after Skip Fowler for Madden's murder?"

51

Cashmere snorted. "You're crazy. Where the hell would you scrape up a posse?"

"The Bench ranchers."

Slowly a smile drew its way across Cashmere's tight mouth, loosening it, bringing warmth into his cool eyes. "That's not a bad idea." He said it thoughtfully as if weighing each word. "Arch Rathbone has this town buffaloed. He's never been whipped, either physically or legally. And last night he made his brag that no one's going to arrest any of his crew."

"Do you think Horn will go along?"

"He will if you handle it right—if you shame him into it. But I wouldn't want the job."

"Neither do I," Moffet said grimly, "but once started this isn't something you can stop."

He turned away from the bar and moved to the door, pausing instinctively to peer over the batwings before he went out into the street. What he saw held him there, motionless. Half a dozen men had ridden up to the livery stable, their horses showing the marks of a long, hard journey. As they halted, Buck Weaver came out of the building. One of the riders stepped down, spoke to Weaver and then shook hands.

The stable was more than a block away, but Moffet had no trouble at all in recognizing the squat broad frame of Joel Champion.

He couldn't forget Champion, any more than Champion could forget him.

Down in Texas, from one end of the border to the other, everybody knew about "Joel Champion," the gunfighter whose real name had gotten lost somewhere along the wavering trail which looped back and forth across half a dozen states and territories and deep into the Mexican wilds.

A saloon man with a sense of humor had given birth to the alias. As a boy, Champion had been a fighter, and the saloon man matched him with a barroom bouncer in a bare-knuckle contest. When the boy emerged victorious, the saloon man dubbed him Joel the Champion, and Joel took it from there.

He shortened the name and lengthened the reputation. He was a killer, by profession and proclivity, deadly as a rattlesnake and as untroubled by conscience. According to a rumor, after he killed one man in a Laredo bar, the body fell across the pool table. And then, legend insisted, Champion pushed the corpse to one side, climbed on the table and lay down to sleep, not a wit disturbed by his bedfellow.

Joel Champion was the most vicious criminal Del Moffet had met during his Ranger service. Three years ago he had seen Champion stand in a Texas courtroom, glaring so balefully that he frightened the faltering jurors into a verdict of Not Guilty. And after the court freed him, Champion had said that some day he would kill Moffet and the other Ranger who had arrested him.

Well, here he was again, ready to kill settlers on this northern range.

Like a rabid wolf turned loose in a schoolyard, Moffet thought, and took a step backward into the deeper shadows of the barroom. Sooner or later he and Joel Champion would meet, and probably only one of them would walk away from the meeting. But this was not the time or the place for a showdown. He heard a noise behind him, glanced around and found Cashmere watching him intently.

"What's the matter?"

"Looks like Rathbone's Texas specials have arrived. They're having a powwow with Buck Weaver in front of the livery stable."

Cashmere came around the bar and peered through the window. "Know which is Champion?"

"The short, heavy-set one, talking to Buck."

The saloon man grunted. "They're turning this way. Maybe they'll come in here. You'd better go out the back door."

Moffet hesitated. Pride wasn't one of his weaknesses, but it went against the Ranger grain to duck the likes of Champion. Cashmere said harshly, "Go on, you fool. There's seven of them."

Moffet gave him a tight grin and let himself out into a littered yard. To his left a flight of stairs led upward, apparently to Cashmere's living quarters above the saloon. To his right an alley-like passage separated the Big Horn from its neighboring building by the space of four feet. He paused, peering through this passage to the street.

He saw the mounted men pull past and dismount at the rail before the saloon. He held his place, and then he heard the voice of Boone Horn call, "Weaver."

Horn appeared in his limited field of vision. He was on the far side of the street, facing the Texans across the dust ribbon.

"Weaver," the old marshal repeated.

The Lazy R foreman was out of Moffet's sight, in front of the saloon, but he heard Weaver growl, "What do you want?"

Horn stood quiet, his old body leaning forward in a half crouch. "Tell your friends to mount up and ride out. They aren't welcome in this town. They'll never be welcome here."

There was a moment's silence, and then a short, hard laugh rang out. "Old man," Joel Champion said, "you've been eating raw meat. Go crawl back into your hole."

Horn's knees bent a little farther. His old hand dangled loosely, close to his gun.

Suddenly Moffet started up the passage. He didn't owe Horn a damn thing, but Horn was the man behind the badge, the man standing alone in the street, backing up the law and set to die. He couldn't let Horn die that way.

Moffet drew both guns as he covered the length of the alley. He found the Texans all facing the other way, watching Horn, ranged in a rough half circle. They were tense, yet smiling, as if they enjoyed the baiting of the old man. Champion had moved forward, as if by so doing he asserted his authority, his right to carry this fight.

"I'll not tell you again," he said. "Crawl back into your hole, old man, and stay there every time I ride to town. The next time I'll kill you on sight."

Horn stayed motionless, his face gaunt, bony in its intensity. Moffet could almost read his thoughts, his resolution to stand there and die. But he did not want the marshal dead. He meant to use Boone Horn.

He said, "Don't turn, anybody."

They stiffened. They did not know who he was or where he was, but they understood the tone.

Horn relaxed a little, a look of unbelieving relief stealing over his lined face. Champion said harshly, "Whoever you are, you're buying a hand you won't like playing."

"Lift your guns one at a time," Moffet told him, "and drop them."

The killer swore deep in his throat, then obeyed.

"Now you, Weaver."

54

"Hell with you," Buck Weaver said.

The gun in Moffet's right hand exploded. The bullet cut through the three inches which separated Buck Weaver's legs and kicked a hole in the thick dust ahead of him.

"Drop them, Weaver."

Buck Weaver dropped them.

"Now the rest of you."

Dust rose in tiny puffs as the guns hit the street.

"All right, on your horses. Ride out and don't come back to Cloud."

Joel Champion turned slowly. His face was heavy, his forehead low. His eyes bugged out, giving him a toad-like expression. As he came all the way around, the toad eyes fairly bulged.

"The Ranger," he said.

Moffet held his guns loosely, casually, one ready to take Champion in the chest, the other in the belly.

"If I'd known it was you—" Champion seemed to strangle. He dropped to one knee, grabbing for one of the guns in the dust. Moffet shifted aim and drove it out of his reach with a careless bullet.

Champion stayed there on his hands and knees for a full minute. Then he lifted himself to his feet.

"I'll kill you for this," he said through the yellow stubs of his broken teeth. "So help me, Ranger, I'll kill you—"

"You said that before," Moffet told him mildly. Then he hardened his tone. "All right, you toothless brats. School's out. You rode up here to help Rathbone, but Rathbone's through. It's open season on all of you. If you're smart you'll get on those horses and drift down the trail. Now, mount up."

They mounted up, leaving their guns in the dust. Their horses made sullen thunder as they went over the bridge.

Boone Horn stepped down almost daintily into the dust and crossed the street to Moffet's side. "Thanks," he said.

Moffet didn't answer. Townspeople began to come out of the stores. They stepped along gingerly, as if the boardwalk were constructed of eggshells.

"You should have killed Champion when he reached for that gun," somebody said.

Moffet turned to find Lew Cashmere in the saloon doorway, a shotgun in his hands. "You'll never have a better chance."

Still Moffet said nothing. He ignored Cashmere, ignored the curious townspeople who had halted to watch from a respectful distance. He stooped, gathered up the scattered guns and stacked them along the edge of the sidewalk.

The marshal didn't offer to help. Since that one word, he had respected Moffet's silence. Moffet straightened, saying in an undertone so that it would not seem to the watchers that he was giving the marshal orders, "Come on down to your office. I want to talk with you."

He saw the question in Horn's eyes, and the hesitation, but then with a shrug the old man led the way to the office. Inside, Moffet checked the single cell to make sure they were alone, while Horn sat down in the desk chair, like a man whose legs were too weary to sustain him. Moffet studied him thoughtfully.

"What made you brace those Texans? It wasn't necessary."

Horn rubbed his lips with the heel of his thumb. "This is my town," he said. "Last night Arch Rathbone pushed me around. This morning I heard people laughing at me."

Pride, Moffet thought. Pride, the last thing an old man gave up. It sustained him, and carried him when everything else was gone. Boone Horn had lived by his belief that he could keep control of this town, and in one careless mo·ment Arch Rathbone had shown him the truth.

So this morning Horn had made his move, alone and helpless, meaning to face down the Texas guns, to go out in one last moment of smoking glory.

He had robbed Horn of that chance, by coming to his aid, by taking the play away from him. The townspeople might forget that Horn had braced the Texans, but they would remember that Moffet had made them drop their guns and ride out of town.

"I'm sorry," Moffet said.

A sudden warmth came up into Horn's haunted eyes, as he realized that Moffet understood. "Don't be," he said. "It was a fool trick, a way of getting myself killed."

"I'll offer you another," Moffet said. "That's what I'm here for. You're hurting because you lost a prisoner. Seems to me the thing to do is get him back."

For an instant Horn's shoulders straightened. Then they sagged again. "Just how would you go about doing that?"

"By riding to the Lazy R and taking him."

Horn laughed. "In your mind you've been calling me a fool for bracing Champion. I'd be a worse fool to ride into the Lazy R."

"Why? You're a deputy sheriff. With a posse at your back you'd have a good chance of taking Fowler."

"And where would I get a posse? You've seen the way this town reacts to trouble, especially trouble caused by Rathbone's men."

"You could use the Bench ranchers. They're spoiling for a crack at the Lazy R. Give them a legal chance to bring in Karl Madden's murderer."

Horn stared at him. "What's your interest in this business, son?"

Moffet told him then. He told it without bitterness, in short, swift sentences. "I've come a long way," he finished. "I'm not going to turn back now."

"No," Horn said, "you're not going to turn back—not until you've settled your score with Rathbone."

Moffet watched him. "You almost sound like you're defending Rathbone."

Horn shook his head. "I'm not defending him, but I've lived a long time. This trouble's been brewing ever since Tom Drake came into the country, and it's partly my fault because I sat quiet and watched it grow. I saw it coming, and yet I closed my mind to it. I said, this isn't my business, it isn't in Cloud, and I was wrong. A man has to live with himself, and I did some thinking after Arch took my prisoner last night. It is my business. I either have to control Cloud and the valley or get out."

"Yes," Moffet said. "I'm aware of that. I'm giving you the chance, Marshal. Ride to the schoolhouse meeting with me tonight."

"No."

Moffet tried to hide his disappointment. "I know you're not refusing because you're scared."

"No. At least I'm not scared the way you mean."

"Then what?"

Horn said, "Look at it this way. You figure you've got a score to settle with Arch. Tom Drake hates him, and the rest of the Bench ranchers hate him. If I ride with you to the Lazy R how do I know you'll arrest Skip Fowler and let it go at that? How do I know you won't burn the ranch and kill Arch in the bargain?"

"If I'd come here just to kill Arch I'd have tried it last night."

"You're still trying to use me as a catspaw."

"I'm offering a trade," Moffet said. "I'm offering to give back your authority in this town in return for your riding with me. Can't you see, Boone, you've lost your hold on Cloud, and you'll never get it back as long as Arch holds power. These gunmen riding for him are only willing to do his dirty work as long as they think he can protect them. They feel no loyalty to the ranch or to him. Now, if we arrest Fowler and bring him here for trial—"

"Not here. To the county seat."

"All right, to the county seat. If we do that, Arch's specials will start wondering which one of them is next. I know how that works. I didn't ride with the Rangers four years for nothing. We brought law into some of the toughest corners of the border country. We didn't arrest every outlaw—we couldn't have because we didn't have enough men. But we put the fear of God into them. We made them believe they'd be healthier away from Texas, and a lot of them pulled out."

The old man was listening.

"That's what I'm going to do to the Lazy R men—make it so hot here that most of them will pull out. Without a crew Arch is just another man. Big, powerful, dangerous, sure. But still only a man."

"All right," Horn said, and stood up suddenly. "Maybe I'm making a mistake, but I'll ride with you. It's the one chance I see of keeping any peace in this valley. But I'm warning you, as soon as you or any one of the Bench ranchers gets out of line I'll act the same as I'm acting toward Arch. I'll come for you, even if I have to deputize the whole Lazy R to do it."

Chapter Nine

The North Bench schoolhouse was built of pole pine logs, with a sod roof. It clung to the slope, a quarter of a mile below the dark line which the timber made as it crept down the shoulders of the higher hills.

The teacher's desk sat on a square raised platform to give her a commanding view of the dozen pupils who normally occupied the room, and their benches ran back in four ordered rows to the big stove which filled the rear corner.

Karen Madden stood on the platform, leaning forward, her knuckled hands resting on the scarred desk top. And, beside Karen's hands on the desk was the case of shells which had caused her father's death.

Everyone in the room turned toward the door as Del Moffet and Boone Horn came in, and a murmur ran through the crowd at sight of the marshal.

A quick look showed Moffet twenty-five or thirty people on the benches and standing around the cold stove, but a good half of these were women and children. It seemed as if the small ranchers had feared to leave their families when they came to the meeting.

Moffet studied the faces as he moved forward to mount the platform. They were grave, scared, angry faces, alike in their intentness, watching him and the marshal with an air of considered suspicion.

He heard Karen introduce him as the man who had come to their assistance, and as the new foreman of her ranch. He saw Tom Drake sitting in the front row, and realized that the men on either side of the big gambler had drawn away, as if they did not quite regard Drake as one of them.

Then Moffet was alone in front of the desk, facing the

group, again sensing their fear and suspicion. "You don't know me," he said, "but I have a score to settle with Arch Rathbone which runs back a long way. I've come three thousand miles to find him, and I'm here tonight to give you a chance to ride with me."

They shifted uneasily but no one spoke. The only sound in the room came from a baby, crying softly in its mother's arms.

He went on, trying to capture their confidence. "You don't know me, but you do know Boone Horn. Some of you may have forgotten that he isn't just the town marshal. He's a deputy sheriff for this county."

Someone at the back of the room called, "Did the Lazy R remember that when they took Skip Fowler away from him last night?"

Moffet said without raising his voice, "That's exactly why I'm here, because the Lazy R did take Skip Fowler away from him. Horn and I intend to ride to Rathbone's ranch tonight and re-arrest Fowler, and we are here asking for volunteers to help us."

There was a murmur. He nodded toward Horn and the old marshal stepped up to his side. He stood spare and gaunt and proud, waiting for the murmur to subside.

It died gradually and he said, "Everything Moffet has told you is true. You people aren't blameless in this fight. I'm not saying you are. But unless some action is taken to reassert the law we'll have nothing here but chaos. You don't know Moffet, and I don't either, but I know this much. He's an ex-Ranger and he knows how to fight. He met Arch Rathbone's gunmen in the street this morning, and he faced them down."

The words had their effect. Every man present had been dreading the arrival of those hired Texas guns.

"So I'm calling on you to ride with us. I'll deputize you, and I'll expect you to obey my orders. We'll arrest Fowler and take him to the county seat for trial, and we'll arrest anyone else who breaks the peace. The law is drawn to protect you, to protect everyone, but it won't work unless you support it."

No one spoke, no one moved. It seemed to Moffet that all the talking had been for nothing. These people hated Rathbone, but they also feared him. They sat, waiting for

60

a miracle to rescue them from the Lazy R, unwilling to take any part themselves. And then the break came.

A man leaning beside the rear window happened to glance sideways. He saw a crimson flame lighting the northern sky, and his sharp, startled cry brought the whole crowd to their feet.

"The Walker, place," he yelled. "The Walker place is burning."

There was a concerted rush for the door. They thronged out into the dark schoolyard.

The flames were distant, a good three or four miles, Moffet judged, but they rose in leaping violence against the black cloud of the sky. Around him, people milled like nervous cattle. At his back, Boone Horn said in a discouraged voice,

"There goes our chance. They'll all see it as an example of what can happen to their own homes. They won't budge now."

"No." Moffet said. "It'll favor us if we make it."

He elbowed his way to the fence and climbed on it.

"All right," he shouted. "Now you have a sample of Arch Rathbone's kind of war. Who will ride with us before it's too late?"

They stared at him, uncertain.

"That fire's no accident." He indicated the flames with a sweeping gesture of his arm. "The Texans got here this morning, and Arch has wasted no time in putting them to work. Do you want to stand idly by while all your homes burn?"

Gar Walker spoke up, a solid man, heavy through the shoulders, with a tight, unhappy face. "If I ride to the Lazy R," Walker said, "I'll burn the hell hole down."

"No you won't," Moffet told him. "If you ride against Rathbone you'll ride as a deputy, and you'll take Horn's orders."

A short man pushed through the crowd. "Come on, let's get home before they burn our places."

Boone Horn had taken no part in the argument, but he made his bid now. "Ride home, Hans Bunker, and you'll ride into twenty Lazy R men. They're on the north Bench. Now's the time to show Rathbone we mean business.

Bunker was a stubborn German. "How do we know how many men Rathbone left at the ranch?"

"We don't. But Arch will be there, I can promise you. Arch didn't order the Walker place burned. Arch doesn't work that way. He probably mentioned it in Buck Weaver's hearing, but he wouldn't order property destroyed. He's too smart for that. If a federal marshal shows up here asking questions, Arch will deny all knowledge of any ranch being burned."

Tom Drake laughed from the crowd's edge, and Moffet turned on the big gambler. "You'll ride with us?"

"I'd rather not," Drake said.

Boone Horn said heavily, "Why? Because you're in love with Arch's girl or because you're afraid? You started this mess, Drake. Now is the time to show which side you're on."

The crowd had put it's full attention on Tom Drake and he flushed angrily under their scrutiny. "I'll ride anywhere you will, Horn."

"Come on, then." Boone Horn latched onto the moment. "Hans, hold up your hand."

Unwillingly the German obeyed.

"I deputize you a special officer of this county. You, Walker?"

Gar Walker said morosely, "What have I got to lose?"

"Hold up your hand." He swore in Walker and then Drake. "That's enough," he said. "If there's too many for five of us to handle there'll be too many for fifteen. I don't want a full fledged war. The rest of you stay here. Keep your families together until we get back. You'll be safer that way."

The unwilling posse rode in silence, and there was a grimness in the way Walker and Hans Bunker pressed ahead which made Horn repeat his caution. "Remember, we arrest Skip Fowler and take him to the county seat. Nothing more."

They did not answer and the night around them was still save for the rush of their horses. They watched the north end of the valley as they cut across its waist, and no more fires appeared to break the deep shadows of the rising hills.

Moffet, at Horn's stirrup, said, "I wonder why they didn't hit another place. From what I know of Champion, he enjoys this kind of work. He loves to pick on the helpless and innocent."

"This was a warning," Horn said. "Arch brought in those gunmen, but he doesn't want a big scale range war. He's smart enough to know that no one gains by a lot of fighting. These Texas guns he hired are a kind of bluff, a way of keeping pressure on the hill ranchers. The very fact that he picked the Walker place to burn proves that."

Moffet squinted at the marshal in the darkness. "I don't follow you."

"Walker lost his wife a few months ago. He never was a strong man, and he's nearly ready to quit. Arch figures he's the weakest link. With Karl Madden dead, if Walker quits the rest of the Bench people will probably pull out peacefully."

"And if we take Fowler?"

Horn laughed tightly. "That," he said, "could change the attitude of the whole valley."

Chapter Ten

Sarah Rathbone sat beside her horse on the high wooded ridge which separated the small canyon of Bunch Creek from the main valley. On this vantage point, she had a sweeping panoramic view of both areas.

Shortly before dark, she had eaten a sandwich from her saddlebag and watched night spread across the valley. She often rode alone. Utterly without personal fear, she found satisfaction in sitting on a high place at dusk, looking out across the broken land which one day would be hers.

She watched the ranch families as they moved from their respective homes to gather for their meeting at the schoolhouse, and then, twisting about, she saw Boone Horn and Del Moffet come up the winding trail from town.

The sight of them puzzled and annoyed her. This was something which she and Tom Drake had failed to include in their calculations. The possibility that the old marshal would take an active hand in valley affairs, hadn't even occurred to them.

Nor was she reassured when she saw her uncle's riders leave the distant ranch and work their way northward along the line of the eastern hills, using the rough ground to mask their passage. She guessed their errand and felt neither shock nor surprise when the leaping flames from the Walker buildings finally lit the night.

She had no sympathy for the Bench ranchers. They were interlopers, thieves and rustlers who clung to the Lazy R flanks like a pack of yapping volves, stealing what they could and whining when they were caught.

To her mind, the upper valley needed the cleansing it would get now that the Texas gunmen had arrived. The fact that the hill people would be driven from their homes bothered her not at all.

She started to turn away, for the valley was a pale silver basin under the light of the moon which had begun to lift above the wooded flank. But then a flurry of movement in the schoolyard below checked her. She stood waiting beside her horse, watching the five men ride out.

She could not distinguish who they were, but from the direction they took she knew their destination. They would be headed for the Lazy R.

It had never crossed her mind, that the northern ranchers would attack the home ranch while the crew was on the Bench. She had to warn Arch, yet she couldn't make it in time. She was a good mile behind the posse when it swung into the long lane leading to the ranch yard.

Horn slacked his pace. He said, "The main house is down beside the creek. The bunkhouse and cook shack are to the right. Drake, cover the bunkhouse, Walker, take care of the cook shack. Bunker, stay with the horses. Moffet and I will take the main house. That's probably where Arch will be."

They came up the short grade and into the ranch yard with no challenge save the barking of the dog. They dropped from their saddles and fanned out quickly to cover their respective posts. A single light showed in the main building and lamps burned in both the bunkhouse and cook shack.

The cook must have thought he heard the Lazy R crew

returning. He stepped out side. He called, "Coffee on the stove," and then he whirled around and tried to run for cover.

Walker halted him with a hoarse shout. Someone appeared in the bunkhouse door, detected trouble in the yard and raised a high, warning yell. He ducked back into the building and squatted there, sheltered by the door frame. He sent a shot at Drake which made the big gambler jump for safety behind the corral fence.

Neither Moffet nor Boone Horn paid any attention. They concentrated on the door of the main house. Suddenly Arch Rathbone's bulk filled the frame.

He wore no shirt and no boots. Plainly he had been ready for bed when the yell sounded from the bunkhouse. Just as plainly, he had no gun.

He stood still, held by unbelieving surprise, staring at the moon-bathed yard. He whirled to dive back into the house, and Moffet stopped him.

"Hold it, Arch."

The owner of the Lazy R towered there, motionless. Then he swung around and walked slowly to the edge of the porch.

"What's all this, Marshal?"

Horn's voice was flat and colorless. "I've come for Skip Fowler, Arch. You must have known I had to come."

"No," Arch said, and he almost seemed to be talking to himself. "I didn't think you would, Boone. I thought you had more sense than to get yourself involved in this."

"You involved me," Horn said. "I never lost a prisoner before in my life. I'm too old to start now."

Rathbone did not seem to hear. He looked around the yard which now was as bright as half-day, and then he centered his attention on Del Moffet.

"You're in bad company, boy."

Moffet said, "I don't think so, Arch. You're the one who decided to travel with bad company. Maybe you heard that I met some of your new hands today. I hope you had enough guns to rearm them when they got here."

Rathbone ignored the taunt. "It isn't your fight," he said. "Get on your horse and ride out while you still can."

"I'll ride out when we have Fowler, not before."

"He isn't here," Rathbone said. "He's with the crew, and

you and your brand-blotting friends had better not be here when they get back."

"Every man in this yard is deputized, Arch. Don't stand against us. We aren't a bunch of riders looking for trouble. We're the law."

Laughter rumbled in the big man's throat. "If this is the best law that can be found on the Crazy Woman, God help us all." He turned to Horn. "You're making a mistake, Boone, tying yourself up to the Bench ranchers."

"I'm tying myself up to no one. I'm a deputy sheriff." The old man spoke in a low tone and there was dignity about him. "I want the man who murdered Karl Madden and I'm going to take him. I have to get my posse where I can, and if I need to I'll put a badge on every rider in the upper valley."

"A bunch of thieving rustlers," Arch Rathbone said on a note of rising temper. "I never thought you'd take their side."

"You forced me, Arch." Boone sounded weary. "I didn't take a hand when this fight started. Maybe I should have, but I thought it a local thing, to be settled between local people with both sides in the wrong. But you changed that, Arch, you changed it by bringing in outside guns. Maybe you don't realize what you've started. Maybe you don't realize that the men you've hired give no loyalty to any-one, that they're as apt to turn against you as they are to carry on your fight. Send them back down the trail before it's too late, before half the people in this valley are dead."

"And if I don't?"

"Then so help me, I'll hang them wherever I find them. Think about it, Arch. You have more than all the rest of the valley people put together. You have more to lose, too, so you're the one who needs the protection of the law most. Stop this fight before it gets out of hand. I've seen range wars before. I tell you, no one ever wins."

Listening to the old marshal, Del Moffet felt a surge of admiration. The big man on the porch was arrogant, bull-headed and utterly unafraid. He had some twenty riders on his payroll, at least six of them trained gunmen. Against this power the old marshal was fighting, not with guns, but with words and with the weight of his personality.

Yet Horn reminded Moffet of a man trying by his own strength to bolster a collapsing dam. Watching Arch Rath-

66

bone's face, he knew that Horn's appeal to reason had failed.

He said, "You're wasting your time, Boone. Arch won't be content until he wrecks himself."

Rathbone laughed suddenly. "That's what you want, isn't it, boy? That's why you rode up the long trail to find me."

"That's right. I judged you, Arch, and I judged you to be a fool. All right, we've talked enough. Where's Fowler?"

"Find him."

Horn raised his voice. "Skip, if that's you in the bunkhouse, come out with your hands up."

There was no answer.

Horn said, "Drake, Bunker, see how many bullets you can put through that building." The first shot cracked through the night, and in that instant Arch Rathbone hurled himself from he edge of the porch. His huge body smashed lean Boone Horn to the ground. The fall and the weight of Rathbone's frame drove the wind out of the old man. He lay on his back, gasping.

Del Moffet charged in, hearing shots behind him, hearing Skip Fowler yell from the bunkhouse. Then he heard nothing, for all his attention was on Rathbone. He seized Arch's massive shoulder and hauled him off the marshal.

Arch seemed to fall backward. His weight broke Moffet's grip. Then Arch swung about, coming to his feet with the quickness of a cat, reaching out and catching Moffet's shirt front, jerking the lighter man forward against him.

Moffet knew what Rathbone was trying to do. He wanted to wrap his big arms around Moffet, to squeeze until the ribs cracked beneath the strain.

He wrenched away, tearing his shirt from Rathbone's grasping fingers, tripping and going over backward as he did so, the guns falling from his holsters as he completed a backward summersault.

Rathbone dived for the nearest gun. His fingers touched it just as Moffet came to his feet and rushed in, aiming a kick at Rathbone's jaw. The toe caught Arch under the chin, snapping his head back so sharply that it seemed his neck must crack. But even as he went over, Rathbone, more by reflex than design, caught the heel of the swinging boot and jerked Moffet's feet out from under him.

They rose together. Rathbone reached out. He caught Moffet by a shoulder and by the crotch. He raised Moffet high in the air and heaved him, so that he landed with stunning force upon the weathered boards of the porch.

The fall shook Del, and for an instant he just lay there. Had Rathbone followed up his advantage then he might have won. But he seemed obsessed with the idea that he had to stop the others from taking Skip Fowler. For that he needed a gun.

He dived again for one of the weapons which had fallen from Moffet's holsters. As he did so, Del rose and vaulted from the porch to land squarely on his back, the force of his jump driving Rathbone's face forward into the hard-packed dirt of the yard.

Rathbone spat dirt. Then with a roar he pushed himself up and deliberately fell backward in an effort to pin the lighter man beneath him.

But Moffet wouldn't allow himself to be trapped. He rolled sidewise and came to his feet as Rathbone rose. This time it was the big man who got up more slowly. For a moment he stood shaking his head like a bull that has been tormented past the point of reason. Then he charged, his powerful arms flailing.

Moffet ducked, side-stepped and buried his right fist in Rathbone's bulging middle. The big man stopped as if he had run into a stone wall. Moffet hit him again in the belly and then crossed his left, sinking it under the heart.

Rathbone's arms found him, and closed about him, but they had lost much of their crushing strength. Del used the full power of his shoulder muscles to break the grip and managed to dance away. Rathbone followed blindly, relentlessly. Moffet hit him in the stomach, on the jaw and in the stomach again.

Rathbone stopped. His arms hung down, as if they were too heavy for him to support. His face twisted with pain. He brought up one hand slowly, not threateningly, and used its back to wipe across his mouth. He stared at Del Moffet in blank stupidity.

"You licked me." There was no anger in him now, only a deep amazement, as if he could not quite credit his senses. "You whipped me."

Boone Horn had risen to his feet, his face gray under its layer of dust. He drew his gun, and his voice cracked with strain as he said, "You're getting old too, Arch."

Del Moffet walked over and picked up his guns. He tested their action and slid them back into their holsters.

Then he realized that sometime during the fight Skip Fowler had surrendered rather than face the bullets which Drake and Bunker were driving through the bunkhouse. Fowler stood flanked by Drake and Bunker, his hands above his shoulders. Still covered by Walker's gun, the cook looked on, wide-eyed and unbelieving.

Rathbone kept wiping his mouth with the back of his hand, and a slight trickle of blood smeared one cheek. He walked heavily toward the prisoner.

"Don't worry, Skip," he said in a labored voice. "They'll never get you to the county seat."

Suddenly there was an urgency about Horn, as if the felt that every minute they lingered here lessened their chances of getting the prisoner away.

He said harshly, "Get Fowler a horse, Bunker. The rest of you mount up."

They obeyed in silence under the sullen eyes of Rathbone and the cook. Neither offered to interfere, neither said a word as the posse and its prisoner rode out of the yard.

Chapter Eleven

Halfway down the lane they halted while Horn roped Fowler's wrists to the saddle horn. Fowler had recovered some of his assurance by then. He was a slight man with a lean face and wicked mouth, a man who never looked anybody squarely in the eye if he could avoid it. But his returning self-confidence took the form of jeering at his captors.

"What's the matter?" he said. "Afraid I'll run off and leave you, Horn?"

The marshal merely grunted and gave the signal for them to ride ahead.

"You heard what Arch said," Fowler snarled. "You'll never live to get me to the county seat, any of you. The crew will be back soon. They'll ride you down, believe me."

Horn paid no attention, but Moffet noticed that it disturbed both Walker and Bunker. Although they had won this round, neither of the Bench ranchers showed any elation. They acted as if the raid had worsened their situation, rather than bettered it.

Tom Drake showed nothing. He rode in silence, not pleased by the course of events in the ranch yard. He had taken a certain pleasure in seeing Rathbone beaten, but it fell far short of his hopes. A beating couldn't substitute for the killing he'd figured on.

He hadn't dared to fire the bullet himself, because the news would get back to Sarah and spoil his chances with the girl.

But why hadn't that fool Moffet shot Rathbone when Arch jumped on the marshal? With Rathbone dead, he could have turned the Texas men lose on the Bench ranchers, telling Sarah the action had to be taken to avenge her uncle. Within three days he and Sarah would have been masters of the whole range. But now . . . well, what now?"

His thoughts crystallized as the posse swung out of the lane into the trail which led toward Cloud. Somehow he had to slip away. He had no intention of accompanying Moffet and Horn and Fowler to the county seat. He had to contact Joel Champion. He had to explain the situation in the valley to Champion. If he could convince Champion that there was more profit in working for Drake than Rathbone . . .

Drake never finished the thought. Boone Horn reined up, and behind them they heard the rush of running horses. The Lazy R crew had returned from the northern bench in time to hear the sounds of battle in the ranch yard, and now they were riding to the rescue.

Skip Fowler raised a long high cry through the night. "Lazy R! Lazy R! Help! Help!"

The running horses passed the turnoff into the ranch and came pounding down upon them.

"We've got to scatter," Boone Horn said, snapping it off fast. "I'll head for town. Moffet, you take Skip through the hills past the old fort and on to the county seat. Walker

70

will show you the way. Drake, Bunker, cut back to the schoolhouse and tell the people what's happened."

He thrust the lead rope of Fowler's horse into Moffet's hand. He said, "If Skip makes another sound, blow him out out of the saddle," and was gone, pounding along the trail toward town. Walker looked quickly across his shoulder, then without a word cut westward across the valley. Moffet followed, while Drake and Bunker swung off the trail bearing north as they headed for the schoolhouse.

Somewhere behind Moffet a gun spoke into the night, and he held his breath, waiting for added fire, afraid that the Lazy R had caught the old marshal. Beside him, Skip Fowler turned his head, and Moffet said in a sharp undertone, "Don't open your mouth or I'll put a bullet in it."

Walked pushed ahead, paying no attention to them, and Moffet had to urge the horses to keep up. The rancher was badly rattled, and Moffet wondered if the man had sense enough left to lead him and the prisoner through the hills.

He listened. The sound of pursuit had died away. Apparently the Lazy R crew was still following Boone Horn toward Cloud.

He called to Walker, who pulled up impatiently.

"Come on," Walker snarled. "Come on, damn it."

"Sure you know where you're going?"

"To the old fort, yes." He rode on and Moffet followed, still leading Skip Fowler's horse. Moffet had no idea how far they had traveled. They were cutting across the heart of the valley, or rather a whole series of creek bottoms where the streams came down out of the hills.

There was no trail, but Walker plunged ahead as if the devil was after him. The man's nerves were completely gone, and Moffet knew that if any of the Rathbone crew caught up with them, Walker would be less than no good in the resulting fight.

They climbed. They reached the shadow of the hills and rode into a canyon whose timbered slopes blocked out most of the light from the moon.

Now Moffet could detect a kind of trail, rough and irregular but still a trail, which looped upward on the shelf, following the windings of the twisting creek. They breasted a small rim and dropped downward into a bowl-like valley. The timber receded and the moon again bathed them in

71

its brilliance, and Moffet saw the dark, blurred outline of distant buildings.

As they came closer the blur resolved itself into the line of an old stockade. They reached it and paralleled it until they reached a gate. The gate stood open, and they rode beneath a weathered crossbar and started across the hard baked square of what had once been the parade. A dog barked and Walker's frightened haloo rang out.

Moffet identified Officers' Row. A light flared in what had been the commanding officer's quarters. Then the door came open and a lantern bobbed on the porch.

"Who it is?" In the lantern light Moffet could see the glint of a rifle barrel but could not make out the man who held it.

"Gar Walker." Walker rode his horse to the porch edge and stepped down. Moffet remained in the saddle, still holding the lead rope of Fowler's horse.

The voice from the porch had a crackling, high sound, like the breaking of dry twigs. "Who's with you, Gar?"

"A stranger," Walker said. "A gunfighter from Texas named Moffet."

Moffet winced. He had never classed himself as a gunfighter. In his mind, the term applied to men like Champion.

The voice from the porch cool and unfriendly. "One of Rathbone's men?"

Walker began fastening his horse. "No, a friend of Horn's. He rode to Rathbone's with us tonight and helped arrest Skip Fowler for Karl Madden's murder. He—he licked Arch with his bare hands."

There was silence on the porch. Then the brittle voice said, "Who's the other man?"

"Skip Fowler. The Lazy R chased us. Horn headed for town to pull them off. He sent us here. We're supposed to go through the hills and hit the county seat road on the other side."

"Step down." It was a command from the porch, and Moffet obeyed. He loosened the rope which held Skip Fowler's wrists to the horn, helped Fowler out of the saddle, then shoved him across the porch into the room beyond.

Once this had been the commanding officer's living room,

but now its walls were lined with crude shelves which held a meager stock of staple goods.

The man with the gun followed them in, and Moffet realized that he was old, perhaps older than Horn. He set the lantern on a counter and propped his rifle against the wall. Then he retrieved the lantern and led them into a large square kitchen.

Here two lamps burned in metal wall brackets, and under their light Moffet had a better chance to study his host. The old man stood his scrutiny, saying in an even voice. "I'm Pete Storm. Tell me about beating Rathbone."

"There's nothing to tell." Moffet ran his hand across his jaw-line, which still ached from Rathbone's blows. "We fought, I licked him."

Pete Storm motioned to a chair in the corner beyond the table. "Put Fowler over there. We won't have to watch him so close." He chuckled, and Moffet noted that his was a wiry oldness, as if the flesh upon his bones had merely dried a little. His face was long and thin, but his blue eyes had a twinkling understanding which didn't quite disappear even when the rest of his expression looked somber.

"Tell me all that happened."

Walker told him, from the meeting in the schoolhouse. Walker seemed to find relief in talking as if it made him forget some of the dark fear that rode him. When he mentioned the burning of his place the old man sucked his teeth to show his sympathy. "Everything gone?"

Walker shrugged, saying in a dispirited voice, "I guess so, but it doesn't matter much now. Nothing matters much. I've made up my mind. I'm getting out of the country. I've had no luck here, and Arch won't forget I rode tonight."

"The Lord will punish Arch Rathbone," Pete Storm said, his voice taking on a singsong quality. "I have warned him for years that he's walking in the way of the transgressor, but the durn fool won't listen."

Moffet stared at him, surprised, and Gar Walker said in explanation, "Pete's by way of being a preacher."

"Not a preacher," the old man corrected him. "Just a man who believes in living with religion the way the Good Book says."

Del Moffet walked over to stand with his back to the stove, warming his hands. Storm turned his attention to the prisoner.

73

"So you finally went and done it, Skip. I knew you was no good, but why'd you have to kill a man like Madden?"

Fowler swore at him.

Storm said, "You're tempting me, Skip. It's lucky for you I've got my religion. Karl Madden was a good friend. I should hang you from the old gate crossbar. That's where we used to hang them. Saw two swing on that gate at the same time, boys that went bad and tried to hold up the paymaster's wagon."

Again Moffet was surprised. "You mean you were in the army?"

Storm's old shoulders straightened. "That's right. I was with Reynolds when we ran into Crazy Horse over on the Powder. Got a hole in my leg, invalided out, but I swore I'd come back to this country. It was me first told Arch Rathbone about the valley. I met him in Dodge, helped drive his heard up here. I was supposed to get a tenth of the increase."

Moffet said nothing, and the old man went on. "But like most of his promises Arch didn't keep that one, so I came back up here. It ain't as good range as the valley, but it's mine. I helped put up these buildings, I don't know why. It never was much of a fort, but some general that never got west of Jefferson Barracks probably thought it'd make a good summer camp."

The twinkle in Storm's old eyes grew more pronounced. "Anyhow it makes me a good home, and I get a little trade from such people back in the hills that don't feel exactly easy in Cloud."

Moffet understood. "I wouldn't think your religion would let you do business with outlaws."

The old man's hatchet-like face was suddenly serious. "Depends on the outlaws. I wouldn't touch Skip Fowler with a ten foot pole, but my kind of religion don't make me a judge of a man that butchers a cow now and then for meat. As long as the hill folks don't trouble me, and have money to pay, I don't task too many questions." He winked and broke off, for the door on the right had been pulled open and Belle Storm stood there, looking in at them.

Moffet lifted his eyes and met her dark ones. He felt a shock and he couldn't explain it. He'd seen this girl just twice. He hadn't exchanged half a dozen words with her.

74

And yet, in a curious way which he did not understand, he seemed to have known her for a long time.

But he saw no recognition in her face. It was almost mask-like as she came slowly into the room.

"They shouldn't be here," she said to Pete.

The old man bridled. "Why not?"

"This trouble isn't our business," she said, her voice low, but filled with deep feeling. "We don't live in the valley. We have nothing in common with the Bench ranchers."

The old man flushed. "They're fighting Arch Rathbone ain't they? Rathbone's an enemy of mine."

"That's silly. He isn't your enemy."

"He cheated me, durn it."

"He's let you live here in the hills."

"Let me!" Pete Storm seemed about to explode. "Girl, to hear you talk you'd think Arch Rathbone built these goldurn hills all by himself. Let me tell you, I was one of the ones that fought the Indians and drove them out, and Arch would never have known this place existed if it wasn't for me. Let me!" He broke off, his face almost purple. "Let me!"

She said, calmly. "You'll make yourself sick. You do, every time you think about Arch Rathbone." And then she left the room, closing the door crisply behind her.

Without any vestige of anger left, Pete said to Moffet, "That's my daughter. Prettiest girl in the country. Don't look much like me, does she?"

Moffet shook his head. "Not much."

"Good reason," the old soldier said. "Pulled her out of a half burned wagon after an Indian attack. Always figured the Lord sent her for me to take care of. She's got a temper." He added the last as if to explain her actions.

No one said anything.

"I'll bet you're hungry." He went to the cupboard and set cold meat, jam and homemade bread upon the table. "Gar, get some plates and cups."

Walker obeyed, and Moffet sat down to eat. He had finished his second cup when the door opened and the girl reappeard. Looking only at Pete, she said, "Sarah Rathbone just rode through the gate."

Pete swore under his breath. "She alone?"

"I didn't see anyone with her."

75

The old soldier threw a glance at Fowler, then at Moffet. "Keep Skip quiet," he said and hurried into the front room which served as the store.

Skip Fowler laughed. "Now you're all in trouble."

Walker's face had gone gray. He said. "If you don't keep quiet I'll beat your murdering brains out." He rose and got a chunk of fire wood from behind the stove. "I mean it, Skip. A man can only be shoved into a corner so many times and then he has to fight."

Chapter Twelve

Sarah Rathbone didn't ride into the Lazy R yard, but she did come close enough to watch the fight between her uncle and Del Moffet. She knew better than to interfere, for she recognized Tom Drake as a member of the posse.

When the possemen pulled out with their prisoner, she drifted back, uncertain as to how to proceed, and paralleled their course as they turned into the trail for Cloud. She wanted a chance to talk to Drake alone, to find out what all this would mean to them. But then she heard the Lazy R crew returning and checked her horse to await developments.

She saw Boone Horn halt his men. She saw them separate. The old marshal continued on toward town. Walker led Moffet and the prisoner off across the valley toward the western hills. But Drake and Bunker were heading north, probably going to the schoolhouse.

She hid in a small clump of timber beside a creek, let them pass, and then spurred after them.

Bunker heard her coming and pounded on. Drake threw a glance over his shoulder, recognized her and hauled up.

"Where'd you come from?"

She looked around quickly. Bunker was gone, lost to sight over the crown of a small rise. "I was following you.

I saw the fight in the yard. I saw you bring Skip out. Where is he now?"

"Moffet's taking him to the old fort, then to the county seat."

"What's this mean to us?"

"I don't know yet," he said grimly. "Moffet hates your uncle and he's out to ruin the Lazy R. He might succeed if he can bring the small ranchers together. Time's running out on us, darling. We've got to move fast."

"How?"

He sighed. "Before Moffet and Horn got to the schoolhouse tonight most of the Bench people were ready to quit. I could have bought out every man in the room."

"Why didn't you?"

He couldn't tell her that he hadn't been ready to buy, that he wanted the fight to continue until her uncle was murdered. But things had changed in the last couple of hours. If he gave the people time, they might organize, heartened by the knowledge that Skip Fowler had been arrested, that Moffet had beaten Arch in his own yard.

"I've got to get to the schoolhouse," he told her. "I've got to talk and talk fast. I've got to warn those people that Arch won't rest now until he's burned every house on the Bench."

"Will they listen to you?"

He grinned in the moonlight. "That's just the point, honey. They won't listen to me. They don't trust me, so I'll tell them to do the opposite to what I want them to do. I'll tell them not to quit, that their best bet is to close ranks behind Moffet. They'll refuse, mainly because they don't like me and don't trust me. I'll pretend to get mad. I'll pretend to try and shame them by offering to buy them out, and they'll grab at the chance.

She shook her head, still not convinced. He told her, "You ride on to the fort. I don't care how you do it, but scare Walker out of guiding Moffet through the hills. The last thing we want right now is to attract the county officials' attention to this valley." He did not wait for her answer. He leaned over and kissed her lightly. Then he spurred away, following the track Bunker had made through the bush.

She watched him go, then turned her horse back across

77

the valley, heading for the mouth of the canyon which led upward to the old fort.

Coming through the gate into the old parade ground, she was relieved to see the horses at the rail before the store, for she had feared that Walker and Moffet would push on with their prisoner without pausing here.

As she pulled up at the rail and stepped down, the front door opened and old Pete appeared. She mounted the porch and faced him.

"I want to talk to Gar Walker," she said.

Pete stood between her and the store doorway, his old body seeming thinner and more gaunt than ever. "He ain't here."

She turned, looking pointedly at the horses.

Pete cleared his throat. "I got some customers, people from back in the hills you wouldn't want to meet."

"You're a liar, Pete." She said this with the easy assumption of long acquaintance. Since childhood she had been coming here to visit Belle. "Let me in."

Pete flushed, recognized the hopelessness of further argument, and stood aside. She entered the kitchen and found the three men seated at the table. Gar Walker and Del Moffet got to their feet. She studied them calmly. From Arch she had gained the habit of command, and she spoke as if she expected to be obeyed. "Get your horse, Skip, and ride out of the country. You're through here."

Fowler started to rise. Moffet said, "Stay where you are."

Fowler settled back in his chair, his eyes bright with anticipation, his wicked twisting into a wolfish grin.

Sarah decided to acknowledge Moffet's presence. "You're a stranger," she said. "You have no interest in this and no authority here."

"I'm a deputy sheriff," he said. "The man is my prisoner. He moves when I tell him to."

She considered him, noting the long, pronounced jaw line, the level eyes. No, he wouldn't obey her. For an instant she thought of drawing the small gun which she wore holstered at her hip, but Pete Storm stood behind her, and she could not be sure what he would do.

"I'm only trying to prevent further trouble," she told Moffet. "You know Arch will never let you get to the county seat."

Moffet regarded her in silence, and she realized that

78

nothing she could say to him would have any effect. She tried Walker next.

"You shouldn't be here, Gar."

"Why not?" he said angrily. "What have I got to lose? You people burned me out tonight."

"I know it. I feel bad about that, so bad that I'll buy your place now. I'll give you three thousand dollars for it."

Walker blinked at her, dumfounded. "You'll give me three thousand? You're joshing."

Sarah Rathbone smiled pityingly. "Get me some paper and ink, Pete."

Pete mumbled inarticulately, but he did it. Sarah sat down, wrote an order on the Miles City bank for three thousand, and handed the still damp paper to Walker. He stared at it stupidly.

Moffet watched him. He didn't doubt that Walker would take the offer, nor was he surprised when Sarah said, "That's conditional on your riding back with me instead of going to the county seat, Gar."

Walker looked at Moffet with a hangdog expression. "You—you see how it is?"

"I see how it is."

Sarah stood up. "It won't be easy to take your prisoner through the hills alone, Moffet. You'd better quit."

He shrugged, and she swung toward the door. "Coming, Gar?"

Walker went without a backward glance. There was silence in the hot kitchen until they heard the thud of hooves as Sarah and Walker rode across the parade.

Then old Pete let his breath out noisily. "They're hard to beat, those Rathbones. They act like they own the world."

Moffet said, "Is there a trail through the hills?"

The old soldier squinted at him. "There must be twenty. That's the trouble. You'll never find the right one."

Skip Fowler laughed. The old man glared at him. "That laugh's going to cost you, Skip. I'll help take you to the county seat myself."

"No!" Quite obviously, Belle Storm had been listening at the door. She pulled it open now and thrust herself into the room. "You aren't going to take any part in this, Pete."

The old man spat at the coal bucket beside the stove. "What makes you think I'm not?"

She was pleading with him, showing more emotion than

Moffet had observed in her before. "This isn't our trouble. You've always said that the valley affairs aren't our business, that we should stay clear of them."

Pete turned away from her but she grasped his shoulder, pulling him back around, forcing him to face her. "Listen to me. Did the Bench ranchers ever do anything for you? They've ignored us. They've treated us like dirt, haven't they?"

Pete shifted his weight from one foot to the other. "I don't like Arch Rathbone."

"And I like Sarah Rathbone. She's the only person in this whole valley who ever acted like I was a human being."

"She's playing a game of her own." The old man growled. "I've warned you about that. I've warned you that the only reason she's made up to you this last year is because she needed someone to ride with, someone to act as a kind of chaperone when she went to see that no-good Drake. Quit talking, Belle. I've made up my mind. I'm going to show Moffet the trail through the hills."

Belle released her grip on Pete's arm and swung to face Moffet. Her black eyes were alive with anger and she seemed to be controlling herself with difficulty.

"I hope you realize what you're doing," she said. "We've lived here for years. We've had to watch ourselves, and not alienate the people in the valley. We've known that the first move on our part that Arch Rathbone considered hostile would result in terrible trouble for us. Think about that, Del Moffet. You're here to stir up trouble. You have a grudge against Rathbone. But has it occurred to you that you might be dragging innocent people into your fight?"

Moffet said, trying to speak calmly, "This is a free country, Belle. You have as much right in it as the Rathbones do. I'd hate to have to live the way you've lived, always afraid I might offend someone."

"It's better to live at peace when you can. I'm asking you for the last time, don't make Pete show you the way through the hills. Don't involve him in your fight."

Suddenly she ran from the room, slamming the door behind her.

Pete spat at the bucket and hit the stove. "Women." He made it sound like a cuss word. "Women, they get all het up and they don't think straight. There's a real war shaping

80

up down below, and I'm old enough to know that a man just can't sit idle when there's a war going on around him. You've got to be on one side or on the other. Arch never did anything but wipe his feet on me. I don't owe him nothing, and if he falls, I'll sleep easier at night." He stomped like an old range bull. "I'll get some grub and a horse and we'll head for round meadows and lay there until daylight. The country above is kind of rough to try and travel in the dark."

Chapter Thirteen

When Tom Drake finally reached the schoolhouse yard he found the Bench ranchers gathered around Hans Bunker, listening to the German's excited description of what had happened at the Lazy R.

"Moffet whipped Rathbone," Bunker was saying. "He licked him so bad, Arch quit."

It didn't seem to register. They stared dumbly. No one ever whipped Rathbone.

"He whipped Arch," Bunker repeated, "and we arrested Skip Fowler and headed for town. But the Lazy R crew must have heard the shots at the ranch, and they came after us. Horn went on, leading them toward town. Moffet and Walker took Fowler up to the old fort. They're going to take him through the hills to the county seat."

"If they get there." It was a man at the back of the crowd, Drake could no tell which. "What do you think those Texas gunmen and Buck Weaver are going to be doing? Once they find out Skip isn't with Horn they'll take the main road to the county seat and cut Moffet off."

The crowd just stood there, bewildered. Drake decided the time had come for him to take a hand.

"I don't know who said that," he said, "but whoever did is a fool."

They turned, murmuring resentfully. None of them liked this big gambler.

"What do you mean, a fool?" Karen Madden demanded.

He made his voice deliberately sarcastic. "What did you hope for? Did you expect the Lazy R to lie down like a tired dog and play dead? Of course they'll try to stop Moffet from reaching the county seat. They don't want to attract attention to the valley. They don't want any more outsiders taking a hand."

They listened.

"But now is the time we have to fight. Arch got licked tonight. Arch isn't going to forget that licking and he'll try to make someone pay for it. So, we have to get organized. We have to be ready with guns when those Texans ride north again."

They stirred unhappily and Bunker said, "It's easy enough for you to tell us what to do, Tom Drake. You've got no women or kids to think about."

Drake's sarcasm grew. "And what do you expect—that Moffet will carry the fight alone? He's only one man. You've either got to band together or give up. Me, I don't like giving up."

Courage is hard to hold. The Bench folk tried to draw courage from each other, but the events of the past twenty-four hours had sapped their resolution. First, Karl Madden was dead, murdered, and if he could be killed any one of them could stop a Lazy R bullet. Second, the Texans had arrived and tonight the Walker place had been burned. Against these happenings the knowledge that Moffet had whipped Rathbone in his own yard shrank to unimportance. Right now the Lazy R crew was hunting Moffet and his prisoner. The Bench ranchers were leaderless, trying to think for themselves, and failing at the job.

Drake gauged their indecision and said with contempt, "All right, do what you will. Run like sheep. But I mean to stay here and fight. I'm not trying to tell you what you should do. I haven't the right to suggest that a man should stay and be killed."

Karen Madden said, "What are you trying to do, Tom Drake—frighten them worse than they are already?"

"That's a stupid thing to say." He walked toward her until only a few feet separated them. "Why should I want to frighten them? I'm fighting Rathbone and you all know

82

it. I've suffered more at his hands than most of you, but I'm stubborn. I won't run from Rathbone or from any man. I'm going to stay and build myself a ranch, and I've got faith enough in my own ability to risk money on the chance. Stay and help me if you've got guts enough."

That stopped Karen, but Bunker said sharply, "Why should we help you? I don't trust you any more than I trust Arch Rathbone."

Drake laughed at him. "Little man, you're in bad shape. You're caught between Rathbone and me, but whether you believe it or not I've got more heart than Rathbone has. Has he offered to buy your place?"

"Of course not," Bunker said, still suspicious. "Are you offering to buy it?"

Drake considered him. "Maybe that's what I should do, buy you out. What would you take for your place tonight, knowing the chances are good that Arch will burn you out tomorrow?"

Karen Madden said, "Don't sell to him, Bunker. Don't you see, that's what he's trying to make you do."

Drake raged inwardly but he didn't let it show.

"Sure, Bunker," he said. "That's what I'm trying to get you to do. Now, let me tell you something. It's been rumored about the valley that I was a gambler, and the rumors are true. I was, and I am. If the price is right I'll buy the land of any man here and gamble that I can hold it. But the price has got to be right, because otherwise, what would there be in it for me?"

Bunker scuffed dirt with his toe. "Let me think about it until tomorrow," he mumbled.

Drake started to turn away. "No sale. Tomorrow will probably be too late. Tonight or never."

Bunker's indecision was terrible to behold. He had worked five years, hard years, for his place, but he was neither a gambler nor a fighter.

"How much will you give?"

Drake appeared to hesitate, but long ago he had estimated the price each rancher would accept when pushed hard enough. "You've got six hundred and forty acres, water, a good house and a fair barn. I haven't too much money but I'll give you three thousand for the lot."

Hans Bunker moaned in anguish. "Three thousand! Why, my cattle alone would bring that on the market."

"Drive them to market then," Drake said.

The German spread his hands helplessly. "You know I can't do that."

Mrs. Bunker pushed forward to her husband's side, two small children clinging to her skirts. She talked in a quick, urgent undertone. Drake walked away. He almost reached the schoolhouse door before Bunker called after him. "Wait."

"Too late," Drake said. "My price has dropped to twenty-five hundred."

A kind of sighing gasp rose from the crowd. The men's faces twisted with anger, and one or two of them fingered their guns. But Mrs. Bunker had had enough. Fear for her husband, for her children, made her lapse into the old heavy guttural accent.

"Ve sell!" she said hoarsely. "Ve sell!"

Drake showed his contempt. "Come into the schoolhouse then and write me a quit-claim. I'll give you an order on the Miles City bank."

A wave of whispering swept the yard behind him, but he paid no attention. He walked into the still lighted room and sat down at the desk, hardly looking up as Bunker joined him.

The rancher was shaking so from anger that he had difficulty in writing the deed. He accepted the sight draft which Drake handed him, staring at it for a long time, then folded it and thrust it into his pocket.

"Robber. I hope Rathbone's men hang you."

Drake grinned. "A word of advice, Hans. Get out of the country as soon as you can."

The German did not answer. Drake said, "You'll thank me for this when you have time to think." He showed amusement, but none of the elation he felt.

The game was breaking into his hands. Next to Karl Madden, this stubborn German had been the nearest thing to a leader the Bench people could claim. Now that Bunker had sold, others were bound to follow.

They came, all right. First Lister, tall and thin, his clothes patched, his boot heels run down. A sandy man with a weak mouth and indecisive eyes, Lister oozed into the room and shambled over to the desk.

"I don't suppose you'd want my place? It's next to Bunker's."

Tom Drake knew very well where Lister's place was. In his mind's eye, the whole valley was mapped and plotted carefully. He yawned.

"Why should I?"

Lister could think of no answer. He removed his broken hat and ran a calloused finger around the stained leather band. "Just thought you might. I'd stay and fight, but I got three kids."

Lister had never found anything or anyone in his whole life. He was shiftless, lazy, and not above slaughtering a cow or calf if he found it in the breaks alone and untended.

"I'll give you five hundred," Drake said.

Lister sputtered a protest. Tom Drake's full lips tightened and his eyes suddenly looked like dark flint. "I'm not running a charity, Lister. Your place is a hog pen. You haven't got a hundred cows and most of those you stole. If it wasn't between Bunker and me I wouldn't gamble a thin dime. Take it or leave it."

He knew before he finished that Lister would take it.

The others came slower, but they came, some cursing him as a thief, others hangdog, grasping the draft he wrote them with hungry fingers. By daylight, with the exception of the Madden place, he held deeds to the whole northern Bench.

He left the schoolhouse, exhausted, and found Karen Madden in the yard.

He halted, surprised, wondering if she had waited so she could sell her place to him. But before he could speak she advanced toward him, a quirt swinging from her wrist by its leather thong, her blue eyes bitter, her mouth tight.

"You're pretty shrewd, aren't you? I listened to the way you talked to these people, playing on their fears. You couldn't have done Arch Rathbone's work better if you'd been on his payroll."

He said coolly, "I'm not working for Rathbone. I'm working for myself."

"I've known that from the first, but I can't yet see your scheme."

"I have no scheme. I just don't like to run, and I don't like people who run."

"So you stripped the Bench. You emptied it. You know Del Moffet intended to band these people together and lead them against Rathbone. You also knew that if he got

85

Skip Fowler to the county seat they would have trusted and followed him."

"I know no such thing," Drake said easily. "That bunch of sheep wouldn't have fought for anyone."

"Even sheep will fight if scared enough. You've robbed Moffet of all support."

"To hell with Moffet. Let him look out for himself. I've tried to make these farmers fight and failed. The valley's better off without them." He smiled. "Are you staying, or do you want me to buy you out too?"

"I'd abandon the place before I sold it to you!"

He said, "Uh-huh," and left her standing there.

Riding directly to his own place, he was surprised to see a horse tied to the corral fence. He approached cautiously until he recognized Sarah Rathbone on the porch. Then he hurried.

She rushed into his arms and kissed him hungrily, ignoring the stubble which the long night had put on his cheeks.

"How'd you make out Tom?"

"They all sold except the Madden girl," he told her as they walked on into the two-room cabin. Coffee was boiling on the stove, filling the dusty room with its aroma.

"I bought from Walker," she said, and described the deal at the fort. "I waited outside to see if Moffet would try the hills alone. He rode out fifteen minutes after I left, with old Pete guiding him."

Tom Drake swore under his breath. "We don't want him to get to the county seat. The game is well within our hands, but if the sheriff comes down here with an outside posse it could still cause us trouble."

"He'll never make it," she said with confidence. "After I left the fort I rode home to the ranch and told Arch all about it. He sent the cook to Cloud after the crew. They have orders to hit the county seat road. They'll know about where Pete and Moffet will have to come out of the hills."

He nodded and poured himself a cup of coffee. He felt bone tired. All he wanted now was sleep. But Sarah seemed as fresh as if she had spent the full night in bed. The vitality of the Rathbones always amazed him.

She asked, "What's our next step?"

He sat down heavily. The next step was Arch Rathbone's death. They had the upper valley in their grasp, but until Rathbone died Drake could never set a foot on Lazy R land. Rathbone had to die, and his death had to be arranged so it couldn't possibly be traced to Tom Drake.

Drake frowned. This was going to take a little doing. With the Bench ranchers clearing out, it would be hard to make Sarah believe that one of them had murdered her father. He almost hoped Moffet would escape the Lazy R crew. Moffet would make a perfect suspect.

He said, "There's nothing we can do at the moment. I'll quit-claim these deeds to you. Then if Arch finds out what's been done before we're ready for him to know, he'll think the land is yours. I had to buy them in my name so the ranchers wouldn't get suspicious."

She nodded. He got a pen and wrote out the deeds, then rose from the table.

"I'd better keep them," he said, "until it's time to use them."

His next step, he thought, would be to get in touch with Joel Champion.

Chapter Fourteen

Del Moffet roused with the first light. It was something he had done instinctively for years, this waking as soon as the day broke. He rolled over and sat up, stiff from his contact with the ground.

Skip Fowler slept a few feet away, his wrists and ankles bound. A rope ran between these bonds and Moffet's ankle, so that any stir the prisoner might make would arouse his captor. Below them, on a cushion of grass, old Pete slept with the abandoned confidence of a baby. A thrown pebble awakened Pete, and as Moffet loosened the rope looped around his ankle, Fowler stirred and sat up.

Half an hour later they headed westward, cutting into some of the roughest country Moffet had ever seen. Fowler rode ahead. They had freed his wrists, and he rode glumly, as if it had finally reached him that his predicament was really serious. The old man talked incessantly, telling Moffet about the country, about the Indian fights he had taken part in, and about his girl Belle.

"Don't know what to do with her," he said. "I pulled her out from that burning wagon and she wrapped her arms around my neck and I've loved her ever since."

"Don't you know who she really is?"

The old man shook his head. "Don't know a thing about her. The wagon was plumb gone, the man and woman in it were dead. Damn fools, trying to cover that trail alone. They were really asking for trouble."

Moffet nodded.

"So I kept her, and I raised her the best I could. The fort's a good place for an old codger like me, but it ain't no place for a growing girl. She needs friends of her own age, and fellows, and a chance to live a normal life."

Pete glanced slyly at Moffet and Moffet grinned in spite of himself.

"Don't look at me, Pete."

"What's the matter with you?"

"Well, first I'm a saddle bum. I own two horses and the clothes I'm wearing and nothing else."

"Shucks, a man don't have to be as rich as Arch Rathbone to amount to something."

"Second, the girl doesn't like me. She's gone out of her way to show it every time we've met."

"That don't mean nothing. Females are a contrary breed. They show they like a man by fighting with him."

Del Moffet laughed. "How many times you been married, Pete?"

"Five."

Moffet stared at him. "Five times? What happened to your wives?"

The old man scratched the thin gray stubble which covered his bony jaw. "Well now, you got me. The first was back at a post in Wisconsin. Never did know what become of her. Run off with the sutler I guess. Next three don't count, being as none of them stayed with me more than a month. The last was in Dodge. I left her there when I come back up the trail with Arch. Next year I went back, not so much to see her, but because I'd left Belle with her. She'd pulled out two weeks before I got there. Belle was staying with the landlady, and they both was some glad to see me."

Moffet said, "From the way you tell it, women aren't very reliable."

"Not the kind that would marry me," Pete admitted, "but then, my Belle's different. I've been thinking some of sending her back East to school. Never seem to get enough money together. She'd make a fine lady."

Moffet changed the subject, but the old man kept coming back to it. "Seems like I got a feeling that something may happen to me. I got to think of the girl."

Moffet said, "Don't fool me, Pete. A tough old piece of leather like you goes on forever. You'll live to be a hundred."

"Could be, but the girl's on my mind. She's not got a real friend in the world."

"What about Sarah Rathbone?"

Pete spat. "Sarah's just like Arch. She's selfish and she's self-centered. If the chips were down she wouldn't do anything for Belle." He broke off, staring away at the distant snow capped peaks.

They were climbing, following a winding canyon that seemed to have no end. It grew colder as they gained altitude. Both Moffet and Fowler shivered with the chill, but Pete appeared unaffected.

They had lost all sign of a trail, and Moffet couldn't help wondering if the old soldier still had any idea where they were going. Twice he almost asked, but finally they topped out of a canyon, came over the crest of the ridge and turned down a narrow draw which paralleled the Crazy Woman on the west side of the first high ridge.

At noon they camped by a small brook that tumbled out of a side canyon with the speed of a millrace. They ate cold biscuits and jerky, rested a while and pushed on.

The country broke into a series of checked ridges which ran across their path in a kind of miniature badland, and then the valley leveled out and they picked up a faint trail leading southwest. Here Pete halted his horse and waited until Moffet came up.

"No point in me going any further," he said. "Just follow the valley down about five miles until this trail runs into the main road from Cloud to the county seat."

"How far is it from there?"

"From the fork, maybe fifty miles. Good luck."

Pete swung his horse, but Moffet said, "Wait."

Pete hauled up.

"I haven't thanked you," Moffet said.

"No need to thank a man for doing what he ought to do. If you get in a bind, head for the fort. I can always hide you out in the hills."

He heeled his horse into motion and rode off the way he had come. Moffet and Fowler watched him go, and then the killer, who had not spoken since the noon meal, said nastily, "You're making a sucker play, Moffet."

Moffet grunted and motioned him ahead. Fowler didn't move. "You'd better listen to me a minute. This was a real grandstand act of yours, riding into the ranch and arresting me, but what is it going to get you?"

"It's might get you a rope collar, Fowler."

"Don't ever believe it. You know I won't be convicted. There were nearly a dozen Lazy R riders in that street. Want to bet that every one of them won't swear I wasn't the man who fired the shot that killed Madden?"

Moffet said, "That part doesn't interest me, Fowler. My aim is to prove to everyone that Arch Rathbone isn't God, and that just because a man rides for him doesn't mean that man is immune from arrest."

Fowler shrugged. He seemed to have recovered from the glumness which had clung to him that morning. He rode ahead, whistling a little as if he, not Moffet, was the captor. The change in the man confused Moffet but made him more watchful.

They moved on, heading into easier country as they dropped downward along the flank of the hills. The sun began to sink in the western sky. It was still only midafternoon, but the high mountains offered a screen behind which the sun would disappear within the hour.

Fowler increased his pace. Moffet called out a warning and Fowler checked his horse.

"You in a hurry to get to jail?" Moffet asked.

"It's better than sleeping on the ground," Fowler said, and something about his twisted grin told Moffet all he needed to know about this new-found cheerfulness. Fowler didn't expect to go to jail. Maybe he'd caught sight of a Lazy R outrider, back along the trail. Maybe he just knew all of the shortcuts and had figured out where and when the

Lazy R would spring an ambush to rescue him from this tight.

Well, he couldn't do his own spotting, with all those rocks and woods around. He'd have to watch Fowler.

Moffet nudged his horse forward until it closed with Fowler's mount. They came over the last hogback, dropped into the cross valley and cut the road from Cloud to the county seat. The road, a mere dust ribbon bearing the marks of horses and wagon wheels, turned almost directly westward.

Ahead, the sun was a red ball hanging above the timber of the distant peaks, its glare hard to see against. Moffet resisted the temptation to strain his eyes, squinting into that blinding blaze. He made himself watch Fowler every minute. He saw Fowler's back arch and stiffen. Then Fowler relaxed and settled into the saddle, leaning forward slightly. He looked loose and limber, yet Moffet realized that inside, Fowler was all bunched together. It was a variant of the gunfighter's crouch, the horse breaker's preliminary slump before he clamped down to meet a tired bronc's last waning burst of bucking. Fowler was set to go into action.

Without thinking about it, relying only on the sixth sense that awakens fully only in the presence of immediate danger, Moffet sank his spurs and lashed down with his quirt. His horse squealed and lurched into a corkscrew frenzy.

And then, out of the sun's glare, the attack came. A dozen bullets cut through the space Moffet had occupied. He lashed with the quirt again and the horse flattened out. He reined left, hard, and the animal crashed into Fowler's mount, knocking it toward the volleying rifles.

Fowler caught one of the bullets aimed at Moffet, and he fell with his foot tangled in the stirrup. His horse began a panicky race for the timber, serving momentarily as a screen between Moffet and the ambushers. Moffet reined left and drove for the shelter of a rocky shoulder.

Bullets splattered rock splinters around him, but he made it into the trees.

Behind him, men shouted and swore as they crashed through the brush. Moffet jerked the rifle from its boot and sent four bullets toward the shouting. He heard a high wild cry as one of them struck home.

Within the timber the shadows had already deepened until it was more than half dark. He pulled away to his right, keeping the noise down by riding around patches of loose rock, and climbed along the slit of a canyon in an effort to reach the ridge and cross into the next valley.

But the canyon pinched, ending in a sharp wall down which a small stream tumbled with the force of a waterfall. He couldn't scale it, so he back-tracked grimly. Del Moffet had been in tight spots before, but death had never come closer. He felt like a fox circled by a pack of yapping dogs, a circle which was closing inexorably.

He had no illusions about what would happen if the Lazy R caught him here. He had fought Weaver in the main street of Cloud. He had licked Rathbone in his own ranch yard. And Joel Champion . . . He didn't want to think of Champion.

Riding with care, he retraced his route, hunting a break in the canyon wall which a horse could climb. The stunted trees grew together with the closeness of a fence, and the soil to which they clung was paper thin, a layer masking the rocky strata beneath.

The only way out seemed to be the mouth of the canyon by which he had entered. He debated leaving the horse and pulling himself upward from tree to tree, using the slender trunks as a sort of vertical-rung ladder to the canyon rim.

But he had the true horseman's fear of being set afoot in a hostile country. He couldn't leave the horse, and the idea of hiding in the canyon until nightfall had even less appeal. The Lazy R would discover the mouth of the canyon before dark, and then he'd really be trapped for keeps.

He pushed on.

He reached the entrance without trouble and started down through the timber, bearing to his left, hunting a way to circle back into the hills without using the track he and Fowler had followed, riding in here.

After a while he came out on a rocky piece of ground which supported no timber. At that instant a horseman appeared from the other edge. The man saw him and went rigid with surprise.

Moffet whipped his rifle up automatically. He fired twice, seeing his bullets strike, seeing the man pitch down and the riderless horse sweep away.

The echo of his shots caused a tumult on the slope. Men yelled at each other, and horses thrashed through the brush. Now he had to go by the valley route. The valley offered the quickest road to the higher hills.

He sent his horse plunging ahead, and the hell with the racket he made. The confusion about him helped. The very number of the Lazy R crew gave him an advantage. They would hesitate to fire at any unidentified noise because it might be one of their own men.

Hearing a crashing on his left, he fired into the brush and drew a burst of shots in return. One nicked his hat brim. Another burned through the horse's mane, hardly breaking the skin beneath but making the animal swerve and almost unseat Moffet.

He rushed on, hit a creek bed and somehow managed to scramble up the sharp farther bank and dive again into the sheltering growth.

Here he reined in quickly, letting the horse blow, feeling the animal tremble under him. He glanced back at the stream they had just crossed. It was nearly dark now, but he caught movement on the far side of the bottom. He threw a shot, then spurred away. He topped another ridge and saw the welcome spread of the wide valley with the trail winding up along its floor.

Behind him the pursuit was bunching. He dropped to the valley and took the trail, shaking up the horse for a long loping run toward the ridges five miles away.

Night closed down, blurring the canyon walls, blotting out sight of his pursuers. He eased the horse. The animal was tired, but so probably were the Lazy R horses. Now that he was in more open country he breathed a little easier.

They couldn't track him in the darkness, but they probably knew the hills. They would follow the valley and go over the crest and to the old fort. He would go the other way.

He climbed steadily, his horse's pace slowing as the sharpness of the grade increased. He stopped urging the animal for the moon had not yet risen and the valley, narrowing now and hemmed in by timber on both flanks, was as dark as a trouser pocket.

As the altitude increased the trees grew farther and

farther down the banks until they hugged the path closely on both sides.

The horse staggered a little. Moffet halted again and dismounted, listening carefully for sounds along the back trail.

He heard none, but they would be coming. He glanced at the sky, having to look almost straight up because of the crowding timber. Then he got some jerked meat from the saddlebag and chewed it as he moved on, leading the horse.

The trees began to thin. The climb was steeper now, and the ridge top was just above timberline. He remounted and pressed on. He wanted to be over the ridge before the moon rose.

The cold wind sucked at him, making him shiver. The steady blast was coming directly off the snow which still blanketed the higher peaks.

He longed to turn into the timber, to find a sheltered nook and light a fire, but he didn't dare. He climbed on. His legs had gained a limp, rubbery feel as if all blood had left them. Now, also, he did not dare to ride. He had to keep walking to hold some little warmth inside his numbed body.

The timber became only an occasional tree, twisted by the constant wind which roared down upon it. The moon came up with incredible swiftness, a glow of light to the eastward, then a half orange, huge and brilliant in the sky, then lifting entirely clear of the horizon to soften the bare rock and throw weird shadows from the grotesque tree trunks.

He reached the crest, puffing from exertion in the thin air, and despite the cold, clammy with sweat.

The trail looped downward into the canyon ahead, twisting like a tortured snake as it made its abrupt descent. He did not follow it, but went along the ridge, keeping above the timberline, working backward and forward across the rocks as he sought a path his horse could follow. They dipped, crossed a rushing stream and began the climb of a barren face which seemed to sweep upward toward the snowy crest.

Halfway up he found a fissure which slanted down to the right, ending in a clump of trees like a dark blob below him.

The horse did not like the footing and followed unwillingly as they dropped five hundred feet to find themselves in a tiny, timbered bowl.

There was no water, but the bowl sheltered them from the wind and Moffet felt sure they couldn't be seen from above. With a sigh he pulled the saddle from the animal and hobbled it. Taking the blanket, he settled down in the softest place he could find, a cranny between the roots where the pine needles made a thicker carpet.

He lay wrapped in the blanket, shivering, trying to get seemed balanced on the sloping side of the bare rock, and enough warmth in his body so sleep would come. But the moon was low and the stars dim before his eyes finally closed and he slept from sheer exhaustion.

Chapter Fifteen

He awoke in full daylight, and lay for a while savoring the warmth of the morning sun. Then he went to his saddlebag, got the last of the jerky and dry biscuits. Lacking water, he chewed stubbornly with the hard-won knowledge that a man should eat when he could.

Afterward he left the horse hobbled and climbed up the steep face. He wanted a vantage point from which he could watch the trail to the old fort.

He found it, a crevice behind a heap of boulders that settled down for his vigil. He waited a long time. The sun was near the zenith when he saw them in the far distance, like ants scattered in a quest for crumbs, searching the country as they moved through it.

They were too far away to recognize, almost too far away to see, and they worked slowly, their horses criss-crossing as they quartered the ground for sight of his passage. They topped the ridge and dropped from sight in the distant canyon, only to reappear on the next ridge as they con-

tinued eastward toward the round valley where he and
old Pete had spent the night.

He was in no hurry to move. He understood this old
game thoroughly. In his time he had searched miles of
rough country, hunting for fugitives. The standard search-
er's trick was to pass by, apparently noticing nothing, only
to double back and wait until the hunted man rode directly into the trap.

Well, he didn't intend to make the typical fugitive's
mistake. In a grim sort of way he found the situation
humorous. In just such a hunt he and four Ranger com-
panions had trapped Joel Champion and his partner and
brought them in. He'd caught them asleep after they
thought the hunt had gone beyond them.

He knew Champion hadn't forgotten the incident.
Champion would circle again and again, watching the
back trail to see if Moffet had been bypassed.

He waited until near dark before he slipped back to his
hobbled horse and led the famished animal to the nearest
water. Later, when the moon was full, he took up his slow,
cautious advance, feeling his way as he rode, studying each
fresh ridge before he climbed it.

But he found nothing alarming in his path, and he
reached the round valley long before morning.

Watering the horse, he debated whether to camp here
until daylight or push on to the fort. He had no food, but
he preferred to wait rather than risk coming upon the
Lazy R in the darkness.

Ten minutes after dawn broke, he mounted up. Now he
rode steadily, with more confidence. The chances were that
the Lazy R had abandoned its search and returned to the
ranch.

But his natural instinct made him pause as he came up
over the last ridge and stared down at the old fort in the
center of the wooded valley. He sat a long time. He
couldn't see the gate. Only a segment of the west wall
showed through the trees.

He saw nothing suspicious, but caution prompted him
to pull off the trail and ride in through the timber, approaching the buildings from the rear.

The soldiers who had built this post had cleared the trees
and brush from around the fort, leaving a thousand-yard

open swath around the buildings. At the clearing's edge, Moffet halted again for another look.

Still he saw no sign of life, no smoke rising from the chimney along the old officers' row, and this very lack alarmed him. It was chilly enough for a fire this morning and under normal conditions a fire would have been visible within the stockade.

Had something happened to Pete and Belle Storm? He rode forward then, not toward the corner which led to the gate, but directly at the wall. Reaching it, he pulled his rifle from its boot and stood up in the saddle, gripping the edge of the log stockade and pulling himself to its top. He sat straddling the wall, rifle ready, studying the buildings across the parade.

He saw no horses at the racks, no movement at all. But the door to the store room stood wide. He turned slowly, looking toward the gate, and then his stomach muscles clinched in a spasm of horror.

A figure dangled from the end of a rope which had been tied to the gate's crossbar. The body swayed a little in the wind, as if a trace of life still remained.

Del Moffet forgot his caution. He vaulted to the hard ground and ran across the parade. Pete Storm hung slackly, his head bent to one side, his neck twisted by the hangman's knot fastened under his left ear.

Before he reached the body Moffet realized that the old man was dead. The movement which he had taken for a convulsive gesture was nothing but the swinging of the body in the downdraft.

He stared up at the old man, his throat tight, a blinding rage threatening to choke him.

He knew what had happened. The Lazy R crew had ridden out of the hills, and he could picture the rest. They had stopped at the fort, probably convinced that Moffet was ahead of them, probably knowing that old Pete had guided him through the hills. There had been an argument, maybe a fight, and they had hanged the old man to the crossbar where he had seen others hanged in the days gone by.

Moffet leaned his rifle against the stockade wall, wondering at the easiest way to cut the body down. Then he remembered the girl, and a stab of quick fear ran through him.

Had she been here when the Lazy R crew arrived? Had she witnessed the hanging, and if so, where was she now?

He found the knife in his pocket and opened it and moved toward the gate, preparing to climb the stockade wall. He stopped as his ears caught the drum of a horse's hoofs on the trail below the fort.

He dropped the knife, caught up his rifle and peered around the gate post, watching the trail as it looped up out of the timber and slanted across toward the gateway.

He saw her break from the brush, her horse running easily, and knew a moment of sweeping relief. Apparently she hadn't been hurt.

But what if she hadn't been here when the Lazy R arrived? What if she didn't know Pete was dead?

He had to stop her. He couldn't let her ride into this horror unwarned. He dropped his rifle and began to run down the trail. He had no idea of what he meant to say. He only felt a desperation, an urge to save her from the shock of grief as long as possible.

She saw him coming and reined up in surprise. And then her eyes went beyond him and saw the form dangling at the end of the rope.

Her hand came up to press tightly against her partly opened lips. She swayed in the saddle before she caught herself and dismounted.

Del Moffet reached out to steady her. They stood close together, both looking at the gate.

Belle's voice had a breathless quality as if she had been running. She said, "Who—why—" and choked, unable to continue.

Moffet told what had happened in a dozen sentences. "But it never occurred to me that they'd come back here and bother old Pete," he concluded.

She drew away then, as if suddenly aware of his hand beneath her elbow, and her voice was bitterness itself.

"It never occurred to you! Nothing occurs to you, Mr. Moffet, except your grudge against Arch Rathbone. You come riding up into this valley with hate in your heart. You want to use the valley people to fight Arch and you don't care who gets hurt."

He flinched under the lash of her tongue. He said, "I didn't bring the gunmen up here. You had quite a war going on before I arrived."

98

"But Pete wasn't in it. You talked Pete into riding through the hills. Pete and I lived here for ten years, just tolerated by the valley people. What part did we have in their fight? Why was it important for Pete to ride with you? What difference did it make to him whether Skip Fowler got to the county seat or not?"

He couldn't answer.

"Pete never knew Karl Madden except to speak to him on the street," she said. "If the positions had been reversed neither Madden nor any other Bench rancher would have raised a finger to bring Pete's murderer to justice. They had nothing but contempt for us."

Her voice broke. She fought visibly for control, then went on in a quieter tone. "You're not fully to blame, I suppose. Pete never could say no to anyone. And it killed him—killed him—" She walked away toward the gate.

Moffet caught her and held her.

"Go on up to the house," he said. "I'll bring him in."

She looked at him out of a face that had been drained of all expression.

"You hold him," she said, and stooped to retrieve Moffet's open knife from the dust. With the lightness of a squirrel she scrambled to the top of the stockade, leaned forward and slashed at the rope where it circled the head beam.

Moffet stood below, his arms around Old Pete's knees. At the third slash of the knife the rope severed and the full weight of the stiffened body dropped into his arms.

Without a word he carried the dead man across the parade and laid him in the long shadow of the porch roof.

The girl went past him into the store. She returned with a blanket, a saw, a hammer and some nails. Silently he took them from her and looked around. She motioned toward an old stable which had partly fallen in, and they walked to it. A small gesture of her head indicated the scarred boards of the old stalls.

He took them apart and constructed a rude box. The girl placed the folded blanket in the box and he carried it to the old cemetery on the hill. Next he carried the old man up the hill, placed him in the homemade coffin, folded the blanket around him and fastened the lid.

He turned to find the girl behind him, already at work

with a shovel. He took it from her and dug the shallow grave.

After the box had been lowered and the dirt replaced, Belle Storm bent her head. Moffet saw her lips move and knew she was praying. When she left the grave she stumbled, and he realized that she was blind with tears.

He caught her to keep her from falling, and steadied her until the paroxysm had passed. Then they walked down the hill to the stockade.

Moffet's horse was grazing listlessly in the bared strip, run out by its last two days in the hills. He caught it, mounted and rode to rope the girl's animal, which had drifted back along the trail. He hitched both to the rack and looked up to find Belle in the store doorway, watching him.

He came across the porch and she said "Have you eaten?"

He shook his head.

She led him back to the kitchen. Already she had built a fire and coffee was heating. He watched as she deftly sliced salt meat into the pan, and then fried some eggs.

They ate without relish, each haunted by regrets, but Moffet could not help noticing and admiring this girl's self-control. He had met few people who could experience the shocks of this morning, and still be realistic enough to accept the necessity that life must go on.

She rose, gathering up the plates, saying in an even voice, "If I'd stayed home this might not have happened."

He was glad that she hadn't been here. He had no illusions about the gallantry of Joel Champion and the men who rode with him.

They were criminals of the lowest order, men listed as the blackest along the border. In their souls not the slightest particle of decency existed, and a lone, defenseless woman would have suffered abuse and worse at their hands.

"Where were you?" he asked.

Her eyes darkened and a shadow seemed to fall across her face. "I was at the Lazy R." She said it as if she despised herself for having to admit it.

"Sarah came here last night and asked me to ride over to Tom Drake's place with her. I hated to leave, not knowing where Pete was, but I owe Sarah a great deal and I

100

couldn't refuse. Then, after she saw Drake it was very late and she insisted that I go back to the ranch with her."

An unspoken question formed in Moffet's mind. The girl answered it with a question of her own, as if she could read his thoughts.

"You don't think that Sarah knew what was going to happen? You don't believe she got me away from here on purpose?"

He said, "I don't know."

"Which means you do believe Sarah drew me away from here deliberately?"

"Probably, to avoid trouble."

She sat down beside the table and for a moment all beauty faded from her elfin face, leaving it bleak and disillusioned and despairing. Strangely, this touched him more than her tears had.

He felt a sudden, deep sense of responsibility for her. Without Pete she was alone, yet pride wouldn't permit her to ask help of anyone. This, coupled with her natural shyness, built one more wall between her and the greater world out beyond the isolated fort and its encircling hills.

He heard her say, "If I can't trust Sarah there's no one I can trust, no one," and wanted to take her into his arms, to hold her and protect her, to shut out her fears. Trouble was, he couldn't do that.

Well, then, what could he say? How could he break down the wall of reserve which stood between them? He told her softly, "I think Pete had a feeling that something was going to happen. He kind of put you in my care."

He could sense that she stiffened. "Your care? I don't need anyone to take care of me."

"Of course you don't," he told her hastily. "But I sort of halfway promised Pete. When I come back—"

"Where are you going?"

He was genuinely surprised. It had been so clear in his own mind that it seemed she should understand. He had known what he must do ever since he found old Pete's body swinging from the crossbar above the gate.

"To the Lazy R," he told her. "To have a showdown with Arch Rathbone."

"To the Lazy R? They'll kill you!"

"Maybe, but it's something that I have to do, Belle. You were right. I rode up into this valley with one purpose in

101

mind—to break Arch Rathbone, to make him crawl on his hands and knees."

Suddenly he realized that the wall behind her eyes was gone.

"I hated him," Moffet went on, "but not because he'd cheated my family." He breathed deeply. "There are few things which hurt a man more than the knowledge that he's believed in somebody and been a fool about it. As a kid I believed in Arch Rathbone, and I was wrong. The very things I admired have made him what he is today. The same qualities, out of control, are behind that bunch of killers he's hired to bring a war into this valley."

She started to speak but he stopped her. "I didn't want to kill Arch when I came here. I could have killed him that first night in Cloud, but I wanted to ruin him, to beat him without killing him."

She said in a small voice, "But you want to kill him now?"

"You can ask that, after seeing what happened to Pete?"

She was silent, brooding.

He said, "If I'd been willing the night Horn and I rode out to the schoolhouse, Pete would still be alive. But I still refused to go the whole way. A man's handicapped if he's still going by the rules while the people on the other side stop at nothing. I know that now, and I don't mean to stop either. I'll ride to the north Bench. I'll recruit the ranchers there and we'll ride to the Lazy R. If Rathbone stands against us, if Rathbone tries to protect the murderers he's got riding for him, Rathbone will have to die."

She said, "You're too late."

"Too late? What—"

"They've pulled out," she told him. "There isn't a family left on the whole north Bench. Karen Madden and Tom Drake are the only ones staying. Tom Drake bought the others out."

He rose and took a turn of the big room. "What is it you're trying to tell me, Belle?"

"I don't quite know. I don't really understand things, I guess, but I heard Sarah and Tom Drake talking last night. I've ridden with her so often that they sometimes don't pay much attention to me. They talk as if they think I'm deaf—or maybe they just don't think I'm important." She said the last words with a kind of subdued resentment, as if she accepted her lack of importance as a fact and no longer resisted it.

Moffet said, "You're worth two of Sarah Rathbone and a hundred of Tom Drake."

She looked at him in surprise, and for an instant all her defenses were down. "You mean that," she said, on a slight note of wonder. "You sound like Pete. He used to lecture me. He said I didn't put a high enough value on myself."

"Of course I mean it." He was impatient with her now. "But what's Drake up to? Buying land on the Bench will do him no good. Arch Rathbone is no respecter of property rights. The fact that Drake has deeds to the land will only make him madder, and Drake has no crew. On the face of it, Drake's gotten rid of the only people who could have sided against Arch."

"I asked Sarah about that. Sarah said the land Drake bought would be transfered to her name. Since she's Rathbone's niece, he wouldn't strike at her."

"Maybe not, but that doesn't help Drake."

The girl shook her dark head. "I didn't think so either, but Sarah said they plan to make a deal with Arch. They'll take the north half of the valley, and Arch the south."

Moffet paced back and forth. "I don't believe it. I mean I don't believe Arch will ever agree to deal with Drake, and I figure Drake is too shrewd to fool himself into counting on it. There's something else, something we're not seeing. The only way Drake could stay in this valley would be if Arch Rathbone died."

"You mean—" Belle faltered. "You mean Sarah and Tom Drake are planning to kill Arch? That can't be so. It's not possible. Sarah Rathbone was my best friend, my only friend. She may be hard and selfish, but in her way she loves Arch."

"More than Drake?"

She twisted her fingers in her lap. She looked down at them and stopped moving altogether.

"Maybe she doesn't know," he said.

"How do you mean?"

He picked up the coffee pot and refilled their cups. "Let's think about it for a minute. Drake's an ex-gambler. He's no cattleman. Yet he bought a small place, and, judging by its looks he hardly bothers to run it."

She toyed with her cup, frowning.

103

"Arch beat him up on the street at Cloud and ordered him out of the country. He didn't try to kill Arch because that would lose him the girl. Instead, he egged his neighbors into a range war. Then, when Arch imported gunmen, Drake bought those neighbors out. Now, suppose this had been his idea from the first—to start trouble, to have Arch harry the neighbors until they'd sell cheaply. After that, if Arch died, he would marry Sarah and between them they would control a cattle empire."

"That's it," she said with conviction. "I wondered what Drake was up to. None of the things he did or said made any sense. Poor Sarah."

He said under his breath, "Poor Arch," and strangely he felt a flash of sympathy for the redheaded giant. Then he thought of something else. "Did you ever hear anything said between Drake and Sarah about the gunmen Arch brought in? Did Drake have anything to do with that?"

She shook her head. "I don't know."

"I wish," he muttered to himself, "I wish I knew whether Drake ever had any dealings with Joel Champion."

He stood up then, frowning down at her. "The question is, what to do with you."

"With me?"

"I can't leave you here alone, not with Champion's men riding the range, not with the outlaws back in the hills."

"I'll be all right."

"No. You've got to go into Cloud and stay there until this is finished." Looking around, he saw paper and the pen with which Walker had written his deed to Sarah. He brought them to the table and penned a note.

"This," he told her as he folded the note, "is to my cousin in Austin. She's the only relative I have. I've asked her to take you and help you get a new life started if anything happens to me."

"Happens to you? What are you going to do?"

"I don't know," he said bleakly. "But I want you to ride in to Cloud. Go and see Lew Cashmere at the Big Horn. I did him a favor when he asked. Tell him I expect one in return. He's to see that you're safe, and if I don't show up within three days he's to sell the pack horse I left at the the livery and advance you enough more money for stage fare to Austin."

"Why should you do this for me?"

He sighed. "I could say I'm doing it because I promised Pete I'd watch out for you, and because I'm responsible for his death. But that isn't the real reason. I'm doing it because I want to, because it's the first thing in my whole life I've really wanted to do. Promise you'll go."

She looked around the big square room. "All right," she said in a weak, small voice. "There's nothing left for me here."

He nodded and walked out through the storeroom. She caught him as he reached his horse.

"Del."

It was the first time she had used his name, and he smiled at her.

"Del, I didn't mean what I said about Pete. Pete could no more have kept from guiding you through the hills than he could have flown. He was that way. He couldn't keep out of things."

"Thanks."

"This isn't your business. You're going to ride to see Drake?"

"That's right," he said, and untied the horse.

"Don't do it. You don't have to do it. Ride out of the country while you can and I'll go with you. I'll go to Austin or anywhere else you say."

The offer brought a swift flood of desire. But that was not for him. "I can't do it," he said.

"Why—why can't you?" She was near tears.

He lifted himself into the saddle and swung the horse about. "Let's say that maybe I'm too much like Pete." He rode off then, across the parade, leaving her a small solitary figure on the old porch.

Chapter Sixteen

In the gathering dusk, Del Moffet turned his horse into the Bar M yard. A lamp burned in the small pole house and smoke curled from the Madden chimney. These were the first signs of life he'd seen since leaving the old fort. The Bench houses he passed had been forlorn and deserted.

Karen Madden came out, holding a rifle and peering toward the corral. "Sing out, who is it?"

"Del Moffet."

She lowered the rifle. "I never expected to see you again," she said. "Come in."

He stepped into the lighted kitchen. He smelled boiling coffee and cooking meat. "What made you think I'd pulled out?"

She placed the rifle in the corner and came back to the stove. "Everyone else has. I'm alone on the Bench."

"Drake?"

She said heavily, "I don't count Drake. If I had the chance I'd put a bullet in him. He owns the whole north end of the valley now."

"If he can hold it."

"Drake's slick," she said. "I heard him talk to the ranchers at the schoolhouse. He wouldn't have bought those ranches unless he had some plan for holding them. Maybe he intends to hire an outside gun crew."

"Or maybe he intends to see Arch Rathbone dead."

She considered that silently, then went back to the stove and filled the plates. She sat down facing him, and he had the fleeting thought that only five hours ago he had sat in the kitchen at the fort, facing Belle.

"You mean he plans to shoot him?"

"He'll arrange it somehow so Sarah can't blame him for Arch's death."

The sudden hate in her voice startled him. "No matter

who, nor how he does it, I'll cheer the man that kills Arch Rathbone."

"Even Drake?"

"Even Drake."

They looked at each other uneasily and then she said, "Before you came back I was planning to do it myself. I was going to ride into the hills above the Lazy R and shoot as many as I could."

He watched Karen's angry eyes, marveling at the difference between her reaction and that of Belle. Not that there was anything soft about the mountain girl. But he could not visualize her cold-bloodedly firing down into a ranch yard.

Karen stiffened suddenly. She came to her feet before Moffet heard the pound of horses on the trail below them. She reached across and blew out the lamp, shrouding the room in darkness. He heard her cross the room and catch up her rifle.

"Who is it?" he whispered.

"Must be the Lazy R. I told you there's no one left in this end of the valley."

"Coming here?" He stood up, wishing he hadn't left his rifle in its boot when he tied his horse to the corral fence.

She didn't answer. She was already moving toward the door. He followed her into the dark night.

They stayed in the deep shadow of the porch, listening. A tiny line of afterglow still showed along the crest of the western hills, but the valley below them lay in full darkness.

From the sound of the still distant hoofbeats, he judged that there were five or six riders. He tried to search out some spot of shelter for Karen but found none.

The house stood on the brink of a small rise above the winding trail that snaked westward past Drake's place and on to Bunker's abandoned ranch.

There was no timber, and not too much brush in which to hide. He turned back, seeing Karen's outline as a darker shadow against the wall. She had lifted her rifle, and he sensed that she wouldn't hide even if he ordered her to. She was waiting, ready, almost eager for a shot at the approaching men. The riders reached the fork where the ranch lane led off from the trail, but they didn't turn in. It took several minutes for Moffet to be certain. He couldn't see them and he had to be guided by sound alone. Then he let his breath out slowly.

"They aren't coming here."

"Drake's, probably." She spoke in a flat tone which held a trace of disappointment, as if she'd primed herself for a showdown and felt let down because it hadn't materialized.

"Lazy R?" Moffet asked.

"Who else, unless I was right about Tom Drake importing a gun crew of his own?"

Moffet said tensely, "You can't stay here alone with riders loose in the valley tonight. Get up your horse and ride into Cloud."

She turned on him. "What are you going to do?"

"Follow them, see who they are. See where they're headed."

"I'll come with you."

"No. I'll have a better chance of not being seen if I'm alone. Go on, ride into Cloud and see Lew Cashmere."

He didn't wait for her answer. He jumped from the porch and ran to his horse. By the time he hit the trail the sound of horses was a faint echo far ahead.

He rode cautiously, halting now and then to listen. He didn't want to catch up with that bunch until he knew who they were.

The dust of their passage was strong in the air. He could trail them by it even if he lost the steady rumble of their horses' hoofs. But each time he paused it came back to him steadily. If this was an attack on Drake's place they certainly weren't bothering to sneak up on him.

Maybe Karen Madden had figured it right. Maybe Drake was importing gunmen of his own to hold the northern half of the valley against Rathbone. Or maybe the men ahead were not riding for Drake's place at all. They could be bound on some mission of their own farther back in the hills.

The moon was only a promise below the eastern horizon, but the night seemed transparent. Moffet halted again and this time he realized that the drumming of hooves had ceased.

He sat, listening intently. They could have heard him and stopped, waiting to find out who it was behind them, or they could have stopped at Drake's. If he remembered correctly the gambler's ranch lay just over the next rise.

He turned off the beaten track of the trail, climbing a brushed slope, slanting between some rocks which crowned the crest. He worked down the other side, careful to keep in the darkest shadow possible.

Below him, the ranch yard, looked ghostly and unreal in the increasing light. Behind the house, timber grew like a dark mat, coming down almost to the corral fence. He swung left, dropping into the protection of the trees. He dismounted, tied his horse and crept toward the yard.

No light showed from the house. The men who had ridden in made a tight group below the corral fence.

Under his breath, Del Moffet cursed the uncertain light. From where he stood the yard was a pattern of grotesque shapes, shadows, making everything unreal and indistinct, and then his eye caught movement from the dark porch. He saw two men step into the hard baked yard. At this distance he still couldn't make out who they were, but the light was growing. Another five minutes, and the moon would be well above the tree-studded heights of the eastern hills.

He waited. One of the men talking in the yard below must be Drake, but who was the second man? And then as the orange disk of the moon lifted higher and higher into the sky, the shadows of the yard slimmed and faded, and Moffet recognized the short, heavy figure of Joel Champion.

He gnawed thoughtfully on his lower lip. What did this meeting between an outlaw and a gambler mean? He wished he dared creep closer, but he couldn't hear the conversation unless he threw all caution away. And as he watched, the meeting broke up. He couldn't be sure but he thought Drake and Champion shook hands. Then Champion walked back down the grade to join his crew at the corral fence.

Tom Drake stayed near the porch, and Moffet wondered whether to follow Champion or remain here and watch Drake. The decision was made for him, when Champion lifted himself into the saddle and Drake walked directly toward the timber.

For an instant Moffet thought he had been spotted, and loosened the gun in his right hand holster. But then Drake veered away, picking up a shovel as he came. He moved to a location on Moffet's right and proceeded to dig.

109

He was so close that Moffet couldn't move without attracting his attention. He kept still, watching Drake dig up something which resembled a box. Champion and his riders had long since ridden away.

He watched Drake drop his shovel, pick up the box and carry it down to the house. From the way the man held the box, Moffet judged that it was light. He saw Drake disappear through the rear door. A match flared and a lamp glowed.

Moffet rose, easing his stiffened muscles. Then his curiosity carried him out of the timber toward the yard below. He moved cautiously, reached the house wall and moved along it until he could peer into the kitchen window.

Drake had his back to the window and his big body obscured the table top from Moffet's view. Moffet watched impatiently until Drake turned part way around. The man had a thick bunch of folded papers in his hand.

Moffet couldn't see what they were, but he tried a guess. Tom Drake had buried the quit-claim deeds he had gotten from the Bench ranchers. Something had happened tonight to make him dig them up. Suddenly Moffet wondered if Arch Rathbone was dead. Maybe that was the news Champion and his riders had brought to Drake's ranch.

He saw Drake cross the room and bend over to blow out the lamp, and he faded back, sprinting silently for the shelter of the timber. He just made it before he heard the rear door open. Drake came out onto the little porch. Moffet crouched in the shadow of the trees, watching Drake cross to one of the sheds.

He reappeared a few moments later, carrying a saddle, and walked to the corral fence. Four horses lifted their heads to look at him, and drifted away. Drake took the coiled rope from the saddle and opened the gate in the pole fence.

He stalked the horses slowly, one hand holding the coiled rope, the other shaking out a small loop. His movements were solid and steady. He worked the horses back into a corner, and as they suddenly tried to dive by him in a flash of hurrying hoofs the loop snaked out to settle about the neck of a big bay.

The bay stopped. The game it had played was an old one, and long experience had taught the horse that it couldn't win once that rope tightened about its neck. The bay followed easily as Drake led it to the gate and looped the rope around the post.

He fitted the bridle into place, then swung up the heavy saddle, fastening the center girth about the neatly folded blanket.

Moffet watched him mount and ride down the lane to the trail. But instead of turning right and following the path of Champion's men, Drake swung left, angling across toward the distant eastern hills.

Puzzled, Moffet dropped back to get his own horse, and then carefully picked his way along the track which Drake had made.

The gambler appeared to be in no hurry, but he rode steadily, like a man with a definite objective. The land was broken, cut by half a dozen small streams, screened here and there by patches of timber.

Moffet kept a long way back, anxious to avoid discovery. Twice he lost Drake, only to see him reappear a few minutes later as he climbed another ridge and sat for a moment outlined in the moonlight.

The night wore on. Moffet figured it must be long past midnight when Drake reached the eastern Bench and climbed it and took a canyon which seemed to lead straight back into the higher hills.

At the canyon's mouth Moffet pulled up, frowning at the narrow twisted track that lay ahead of him. He didn't know the country to the east, and he couldn't imagine where Drake was heading, unless he was running out.

He dismissed the thought. Drake had no reason to light out this way. Even if Champion had brought him a warning to leave the country, he certainly would take along some of his personal possessions, and he wouldn't leave three horses in the corral.

No, Drake was riding into these hills with another purpose in mind. Drake was the key to everything which had happened in the valley, and Moffet had to find out what the man meant to do next.

The canyon could well be a trap. Drake might hide and wait for him behind one of the sharp, narrow turns. He was taking a chance, but he'd been taking chances for several years. He nudged his horse and entered the canyon.

Chapter Seventeen

The route led upward, and the canyon narrowed as he climbed, so that in places he had to ride through the boulder strewn bed of the swiftly running stream.

He advanced with slow care. The canyon was perhaps two hundred feet deep, and the bottom lay in such thick shadow that he had trouble seeing where he was going.

He stopped, listened for sounds from above, and heard none. He eased ahead, holding a gun ready in his left hand.

The canyon floor pitched sharply upward and brought him out finally on a hogback ridge which slanted off to the right. He followed this because it was impossible to go the other way, and topped out onto another ridge above a canyon which looked like a thin slit cut in the troubled earth.

He hesitated, peering around him, keeping in the shadow of some rocks. The sky had paled and the suggestion of false dawn appeared in the east, enough to kill most of the moonglow which had given him light.

And then he caught movement on a ridge a good quarter of a mile distant. He saw a horse and rider emerge, cross the ridge and vanish as they cut downward into yet another canyon.

He went on again. Drake had swung southward following the line of hills at the base of which stood the Lazy R house and sheds, and for the first time Moffet guessed that Drake was headed for the Rathbone place.

The gambler had taken anything but a direct route. He had made a loop, riding most of the night, in order to come down on the ranch from the rear. Moffet wasn't too familiar with the terrain behind the ranch—his one visit had been chock full of fighting Arch—but he did remember that the hills rose abruptly, close to the house, and towered above it.

Maybe Drake had a rendezvous with Sarah in these hills.

But dawn seemed an odd hour for a man to meet his girl.

He sat still, debating whether to follow Drake further or to drop back down to the valley floor. Ten minutes later, he still didn't know what to do. With full light coming on he could be spotted too easily. And then he heard the sharp explosion from the rifle. He jumped his horse forward without thought. He came up over the shoulder of the ridge and saw the Lazy R, spread out below him in the growing day.

The rifle spoke again and yet again. The hidden marksman was on his left where the hill bellied out into the canyon, almost directly above the ranch buildings.

A startled howl echoed through the surrounding hills as one of the bullets knocked the pane from the bunkhouse window. Then shouts and yells rose to punctuate the steady, machine-like fire of the rifle.

The marksman paused to reload.

Men tumbled out of the bunkhouse door. A fresh hail of bullets splattered the dust at their feet and drove them back. The reappeared at the rear corner of the building and Moffet guessed they'd climbed out through a rear window, hidden from Drake's view.

Moffet twisted in another effort to catch sight of Drake, and failed. The brush along the canyon rim was too high. He turned again to stare down at the ranch yard. Strange. Aside from breaking a few windows, Drake did not seem to be trying to hit anything.

The men behind the bunkhouse broke out toward the corral, bent double, racing for their horses. Then the bunkhouse door opened and Joel Champion stepped out.

He stood carelessly, ignoring the rain of bullets from the rim, and he stood alone, holding a rifle. The rest of the crew had reached the horses and the animals were milling wildly, blanketing the corral in a haze of dust smoke.

Then Moffet detected movement on the porch of the main house. Arch Rathbone must be there, sheltered from the fire by the overhanging roof.

Rathbone stepped down to ground level. Moffet saw him turn and look up toward the rim, and suddenly he wanted to cry a warning. But even that would have been too late. Champion brought his rifle up fast and put three bullets into the redheaded giant.

The act had the grace of perfect timing, for Champion, standing close before the bunkhouse door, could not be seen by the crew milling around the corral. In fact, he could not be seen by anyone except the two watchers on the rim.

He ran forward, squatted for an instant at Arch Rathbone's side, and then straightened. He yelled to the men in the corral, then pointed the rifle upward and emptied it at the canyon.

The lone return shot struck the dust a good twenty feet to Champion's right, just as two men who had caught their horses rode around the bunkhouse and pulled up beside Arch Rathbone's body.

There was a crashing in the brush. Tom Drake's horse broke into the open, heading back into the hills.

Moffet jerked up his rifle and sent a bullet after Drake. Knowing he'd missed, he swung his mount in pursuit. He still felt dazed, but the pattern of action was plain. Drake held the deeds to the north end of the valley, but he could move no farther while Arch Rathbone lived. With the Bench ranchers gone he lacked obvious suspects to blame the murder on, so this morning attack had been a diversion, a way to attract the crew's attention while Joel Champion killed Arch.

Moffet's lips thinned. They'd undoubtedly picked a scapegoat, a man who could easily be charged with the attack on the ranch, and he didn't doubt that scapegoat would be Del Moffet. They would charge him with Arch's murder, and they would hunt him from one end of the valley to the other.

He hauled up a moment to listen. He couldn't hear Drake ahead of him, and he had small hope of catching the gambler in this broken territory. Drake probably knew the ground thoroughly, and he didn't.

Nor could he turn back. The Lazy R would be in the saddle now, ready to take up the chase. The smartest move would be to get out of the country as fast as his horse would carry him. He'd come up the trail to punish Rathbone, and Rathbone had received the punishment of death.

Yet with this thought a curious anger came up through him. He'd hated Rathbone, but that hate had been built upon the solid foundation of early love, a respect such as he'd never given to any other man.

Rathbone was dead, shot down in his own yard, shot in the back by a man he had trusted. Whatever his faults, Arch Rathbone had deserved a better fate than that. He'd been a fighter and he should have died a fighter, matching bullets with his enemy.

Rathbone had been out-maneuvered by a cheat, murdered at the orders of a man who hoped to step into his shoes. Moffet knew nothing but contempt for Drake, and he muttered aloud without realizing that he had spoken, "I'll not go yet, Arch. I'll not go until I've settled with him."

He rode along the ridge. He had one idea now—to get into the high country, to reach a spot as far removed from the Lazy R as possible.

At noon he paused to rest his horse in a small canyon. He climbed to a natural fort made by some bare rock walls, and took a look at the country through which he had passed.

He judged that he'd come a good ten miles from the ranch and that he'd shaken off his pursuers. They'd still be hunting him, but he was less worried about them than he was curious as to where Tom Drake had gone.

Studying the country, he thought he saw three riders far back in the broken land through which he'd traveled, but he couldn't be sure. He turned slowly, exploring the stretches to the south and east, and blinked in surprise because he seemed to be looking down on Cloud.

The town must be a full fifteen miles away, maybe twenty, yet on this high ridge he could peer over the intervening miles of hills and see it nestling in the crystal clearness of the morning air.

A trail, a faint line made by game rather than stock, ran in this direction, and he knew with sudden certainty that Tom Drake had gone that way. He moved back down to his horse and mounted. He had no clear plan. He only knew that he must find Drake and somehow keep the man from reaping the profit of his treachery. It wouldn't be easy. Once in Cloud, Drake would have Sarah Rathbone's men to defend him, with Champion's killers as an extra guard.

He set his mouth grimly and shook up the horse. When he left Texas he couldn't see the end of the trail. He still couldn't see it, but right now it seemed too damn close.

Chapter Eighteen

Buck Weaver swung down from his saddle. He knelt beside Arch Rathbone's body and swallowed to keep the tears from flowing into his eyes.

Weaver was not an imaginative man, nor a sentimental one. His world had been a hard one, and to hold the job of riding boss for Arch Rathbone, a man needed to be tough.

But this moment was the toughest he'd known in his fifty years. It wasn't love he'd felt for the big man, but a deep respect for his strength, for his ruthless toughness. And suddenly it was all gone, and he felt like an inexperienced colt that has been broken to a lead rope and then suddenly turned loose. For nearly ten years his every thought had originated in the big rancher's head, and now he felt utterly helpless.

He shook his fist at the high canyon rim from which the shots had come, and Joel Champion watched this, his stubbled lips slightly parted in a grin.

Weaver swung around and saw the outlaw. "What are you standing there for?" he snarled. "Get your horse and go after him."

"Who?" Champion wiped his mouth with the back of his hand.

"Who do you think?" Weaver yelled. "That brushjumper, Moffet. Who else would it be?"

"I don't know them hills," Champion said. "A man could ride off and lose me quick. Maybe you'd better go."

Weaver didn't like this gunman. He'd been willing enough for Arch Rathbone to bring in extra hands at the time when it looked as if the northern ranchers would make a fight of it. But Champion was too independent for his taste.

He said flatly, "You can ride or you can draw your time.

I've got to take Arch's body into town. I've got to tell Miss Sarah what's happened."

Champion didn't care what became of Arch's body and he cared less about Sarah Rathbone. He'd made his deal with Tom Drake. He expected Drake to take over the ranch and he expected to take over Weaver's job. It was the price Drake had agreed to pay for the murder of Rathbone.

He looked at Buck Weaver with chill eyes, and he said, "I've killed men for less than that."

Weaver had never backed down from any man in his whole life, but Arch's death had washed off some of his self-confidence, and all he could see ahead was a very uncertain future. He'd liked Sarah Rathbone as a child, but after she took up with Tom Drake, contrary to her uncle's wishes, a coldness had developed between him and Sarah.

He muttered, "This is no time to fight among ourselves. I'll send some of the other men."

"Not my boys." Champion paraded his insolence. It was not in him to consider any man his equal. Before those whose favor he curried, he crawled; toward all others he turned an arrogant, unreasoning, groundless pride.

Buck Weaver didn't even answer. The whole crew had gathered. He gave his orders rapidly, directing eight men to search the hills and three to accompany him to town.

They hitched a team to a wagon and lifted Arch's blanket-covered body into it. Then Weaver began his long ride to Cloud, with the cook driving, his two men riding behind the wagon.

Champion and his gunfighters rode on ahead. Buck Weaver hoped fervently that he had seen the last of them, but something in Champion's manner made him uneasy. The outlaw was too cocky. He acted as if he owned the Lazy R.

The wagon came down the long grade and lumbered across the bridge. It passed the Cloud store and halted in front of the furniture and undertaking establishment. Weaver told his men to carry Arch's body inside, and went on toward the hotel.

Sarah had spent the night in town. He was glad she hadn't been at the ranch during the attack, but he took no pleasure in his present errand.

As he rode up the street he saw the Champion crew's horses tied at the Big Horn hitch-rail and guessed that they would be inside. He noticed the scarcity of people on the boardwalk. That meant the townsfolk were trying to keep out of the way, and he thought grimly of the last time Champion and his men had ridden in here, and the orders Boone Horn had given them. But there was no sign of the old marshal. Horn seemed content to remain out of sight.

Weaver stepped down from the saddle before the hotel, fastened the horse and climbed the stairs. Through the side window he had a momentary view of Sarah Rathbone, talking to Al Chase. He walked in and the girl looked up at him in surprise.

"Why, Buck! What brings you to town?"

He was a blunt man. He knew no easy way to tell his news and he made no effort to find one. "Arch is dead," he said, and watched the high color drain from under her even tan. "Someone shot up the ranch at daylight. He killed Arch as Arch stepped out into the yard."

She put out one hand on the tall desk to steady herself. The knuckles of the hand showed white under the brown skin as she held onto the desk edge, but almost none of her feeling crept through into her voice.

"Who did it?"

"That brushjumper, Moffet. Who else?"

"No!" The protest came from the far side of the room. Weaver turned his head and saw Belle Storm get up suddenly from a deep chair.

Weaver stared at Belle Storm. Weaver had never liked old Pete. He figured the old coot wasn't above eating Lazy R beef, and now some of his dislike rubbed off on this girl. He'd never understood her anyway. She was too quiet.

"You saw him?" Sarah asked.

Weaver shoved his hat far back on his dark head. "He was up on the ridge, and who else would pepper the ranch? All those bush people have pulled out."

"Maybe one of them sneaked back," Bell said, walking toward him, her small hands on her hips. "Or maybe it's Karen Madden. You murdered her father, remember."

Weaver flushed. He wished he could slap her. If Sarah wasn't here, he would slap her.

Sarah said, "Karen Madden came into town late last night, Belle, after you went to bed. As far as I know she's been in her room all day."

Belle faltered, then braced herself.

"Del Moffet wouldn't do anything like that," she said firmly.

Sarah eyed her with sharpened curiosity, and Belle's throat and cheeks burned. She walked back to her chair and sat down, burying her small chin in her hand, lowering her eyes and brooding.

At any other time Sarah might have laughed. She had never seen Belle display interest in any man, and it struck her as funny that the mountain girl should show emotion over a saddle tramp. But she could not laugh today. The shock of Arch's death numbed all other feeling. She said to Weaver, "Where is he—Arch, I mean?"

"At the undertaker's."

She started for the door and Weaver fell in step behind her. On the porch he said urgently, "There's something I have to talk to you about."

"Not now."

"Yes, now," he said, and Sarah stopped.

"It's those gunmen from Texas. I ordered Champion out into the hills with the rest of the crew. He wouldn't go."

She looked at the horses in front of the saloon. She'd seen the outlaws ride in a few minutes ago. "Tell me," she said, "was it you or Champion who hung Pete?"

Weaver scuffed at the porch boards with his boot toe. "It was Champion. We came into the fort and I went out, circling around, looking for Moffet's tracks. I don't know what actually happened, but I got back just after they strung him up. They claim he took a poke at Champion."

Sarah bit her lip. She made up her mind.

"Get some money from Cashmere," she said, sounding like Arch. "Pay them off. The Bench is clear. Give them until sundown to be out of the valley."

Buck Weaver didn't lift his eyes. "I only brought two of the regular crew and the cook with me," he said. "The others are out in the hills hunting for Moffet."

She understood at once. "You mean they won't go?"

He shrugged. "Maybe yes, maybe no. Champion ain't a man that takes orders."

Her mouth tightened. She was a Rathbone, and this was her town, her valley. "See Boone Horn," she said, and left the foreman to stare unhappily after her as she marched down the street to the furniture store.

Belle Storm watched them through the hotel window and

119

then walked over to the desk. "Which room is Karen Madden in?" she asked in a low voice.

Al Chase told her. She climbed the stairs and knocked on the door of number five. She felt no grief over Arch Rathbone's death, and as for Sarah, she had reached a compromise. She still blamed Sarah for luring her away from the fort, but she didn't blame Sarah for Pete's death. The weary miles from the old fort had given her a chance to think. Sarah couldn't have known that her crew would hang the old man, and couldn't have prevented it if she had known.

Finally she'd taken the measure of Sarah's selfishness and accepted it. She'd tolerated Sarah's comfort last night when she rode into town and found the older girl at the hotel, but now she could offer no comfort in return.

She heard the key being turned, and Karen Madden pulled the door open. Karen stared at Belle as if she had never seen her before, then said in an unbending voice, "What do you want?"

"A minute's talk with you." Belle stepped into the room and Karen gave way grudgingly.

"I don't know what we have to talk about."

"Several things. Arch Rathbone is dead and the Lazy R crew is hunting Moffet through the hills."

Karen's eyes went wide with surprise. "You mean he shot Arch?"

"Buck Weaver believes so, and Sarah apparently does. I can't. Moffet isn't the kind to sit up on a rim and shoot down into buildings where people are sleeping. If he decided to kill Rathbone he'd meet him face to face."

Karen tried to absorb the news. Rathbone dead? Rathbone, who had towered over this valley like an evil force . . . the enormous strength vanished, the roaring voice stilled? She could scarcely believe it.

Belle said, "Moffet left the fort to ride to your place. Did you see him?"

Karen nodded slowly. She didn't trust Belle. Belle was a friend of Sarah's. But Moffet had told her about old Pete's death, and that probably made a difference. She said, "What is Moffet to you?" and saw Belle's face flame and stared at her in fresh amazement.

Belle spoke with an effort. "You did see him then?"

"Yes. He came to the ranch for supper. While we were
120

eating some men rode past along the trail and he followed them."

"Who were they?"

"I don't know. Moffet ordered me to come into town, so I came."

"He's in trouble," Belle said. "The Lazy R is hunting for him. I don't know what to do."

Karen Madden didn't know what to do either. She said, "Wait until I finish dressing," and hastily donned the rest of her clothes.

She led the way along the hall and down the stairs.

At the desk she obtained paper and a pen. She sat down to write, chewing the pen stem as she tried to work out what she wanted to say. She finished the note and carried it back to the desk.

"Take this over and give it to Mr. Cashmere, please."

Surprise washed across Al Chase's bony face. He started to smile knowingly but the smile froze as he met Karen's level eyes. He took the note and hurried the length of the lobby and went down the steps jerkily, his pipestem legs seemingly unable to bear his weight.

Belle concealed her surprise. "What are you writing to Lew Cashmere for?"

Karen's expression was indrawn and secretive.

"Moffet told me to. Cashmere is his friend." She ran the tip of her tongue thoughtfully over her full lips, then said, "We'd better go see Boone Horn," and led Belle out onto the sidewalk as Al Chase disappeared into the Big Horn.

The Big Horn's long room seemed strangely quiet. Joel Champion and his men sat at one of the side tables, passing a bottle back and forth. Other customers who had been at the bar when the gunmen arrived had long since found an excuse to slip away. A single bartender loitered at the middle of the long counter, careful not to look at the outlaws bunched around their table. Lew Cashmere sat at the rear, absently riffling a deck of cards, watching every move Champion's men made.

The riders glanced at Chase as he came in, then showed no further interest. He glided the length of the bar without once looking in their direction. He slid into a seat opposite Cashmere and wordlessly pushed the folded note across the card table.

Lew Cashmere read it without change of expression. He

raised a finger in signal and the bartender brought a drink which Chase downed at a gulp. Then Cashmere rose without speaking, left the building by the rear door, and walked up the street to the marshal's office.

He found the two girls waiting for him, and he was still there an hour later when Tom Drake brought his big bay down the twisting grade into town. No one in Boone Horn's office had yet thought of a workable plan.

Drake came across the bridge and turned into Cloud's main street. The long slanting rays of the late afternoon sun threw a reaching shadow from the moving rider across the trampled dust. Drake was a big man and the sun was low, and the shadow stretched the width of the street as if to prove that now Tom Drake was the valley's king.

He saw the horses grouped before the Big Horn and guessed that they belonged to Champion's men. His lips, prickly with their stubby twenty-four hour beard, curved a little. He'd planned this carefully, even talking Sarah into remaining in town last night so she wouldn't be at the ranch when he launched the attack on Arch.

He'd promised to meet her in town last night, and now he had to come up with a story she'd believe, a good reason for his failure to keep that appointment.

He pulled up before the hotel, stepped down, and paused for a moment to admire the way his shadow ran away from him until the outline of his bell crowned hat touched the edge of the farther sidewalk.

He'd won. He'd gambled for high stakes and won, but no elation showed in his face. A nagging worry had ridden with him through the hills all day, making him double back now and again to see if anyone followed.

Who had been on the rim with him when he had thrown the shots into the Lazy R yard? Who had fired at him from the brush along the canyon top as he spurred away?

He frowned at the memory. Had the man on the rim seen him closely enough to identify him? Had the man seen Champion shoot Arch?

He put the questions away from him. As a gambler he'd taken his chances with marked cards, shaved decks and thimble rigs. He'd taken a bigger chance this morning and so far the game was fully in his hands.

He fastened his horse, ducked under the rail, climbed the hotel steps and went into the lobby. Al Chase was standing on a small table, cleaning the big center lamp which swung from the beamed ceiling. When he saw Drake his eyes brightened with malice, and dislike and curiosity. Like most of Cloud's citizens he had little use for the big gambler.

Drake said, "Sarah Rathbone around?"

"She's still down at the undertaker's."

Drake pretended a great surprise. "Undertaker's?"

Chase replaced the lamp chimney before he answered. "Arch was murdered this morning. Buck Weaver brought his body in."

Tom Drake swore in the tone of a man who is utterly shocked. He stood for a minute as if surprise had robbed him of the power of locomotion, then strode heavily out of the hotel. He went on to the furniture store and entered. He saw Buck Weaver leaning against the rear wall of the gloomy room, saw the quick hostility and fear on the foreman's face.

He'd better get rid of Weaver as soon as possible. Get rid of Arch's whole crew, as a matter of fact. They hated him because they thought he'd led the Bench ranchers in the fight. Luckily, he had Champion all ready to take over.

He pushed by Weaver without speaking. He went into the rear room and found Sarah standing quietly beside her uncle's body.

Even in death Arch Rathbone retained some of his commanding power, and Drake gazed at him with a kind of fascination. He had hated Rathbone as he had hated no other man. Rathbone had broken his pride, and he gloried in seeing the man dead. He had an almost overpowering impulse to spit on the bearded face. He fought it down with visible effort.

For once in her adult life, Sarah Rathbone needed comfort and support. She came into his arms, and he held her tightly, kissing her, murmuring wordless sounds of sympathy.

It's going to be all right, he thought. I've won. I've won. And aloud he asked, "What happened? Who killed Arch?"

She told him about the attack on the ranch, as Buck Weaver had outlined it to her, and added finally, "I thought better of Moffet than that. I thought he'd fight face to face."

Moffet! The name leaped into Drake's consciousness.

Had it been Moffet behind him on the rim? He held his tone level with difficulty.

"Did they catch him? Did any of them see him?"

She shook her head. "The crew is still in the hills, searching, and that brings up something else. Something I need your help to do."

"Anything," he said. "Anything."

"I've given Weaver orders to fire Champion. Champion refused to join the search in the hills. He brought his men to town."

"I see." Drake considered this new situation, and he didn't like it. He wanted no trouble with Weaver now, no trouble with anyone until he had things in tighter control.

He said, "Is that wise? We'll need every man we've got to find Moffet, if he's still in the country."

She stepped back at that. "What makes you think he isn't in the country?"

Drake shrugged. "I didn't say he wasn't. But consider for yourself. He came up here to get even with Arch. He's killed him, so that part's finished. Certainly he has no hope of getting back the money he claims Arch stole from his family."

"Well—"

"So why should he stay when he knows every Lazy R hand is hunting him? It doesn't make sense, Sarah. He has no ties here, no interest."

She thought of Belle Storm's defense of Moffet, then dismissed it. She reverted to the problem of Joel Champion.

"We've got to get rid of those outlaws, and do it right away."

He hesitated. He didn't want to argue with her yet. His position wasn't strong enough. But he had to turn this threat aside somehow.

He said, "Why worry about them? They've only done what your uncle brought them up the trail to do."

"They hung Pete Storm. Arch was furious when he heard. He always liked Pete."

He made a half despairing gesture with his hands. "You know how Pete was. He always asked for trouble. He probably goaded Champion until they hung him."

"All right," she said wearily. "It can wait. Take me back to the hotel. I'm tired."

Buck Weaver was still in the front room, waiting, shifting uneasily from one foot to the other, gnawing at the end of his drooping mustache.

"Miss Sarah, can I talk to you a minute, alone?"

She said without interest, "You can talk freely in front of Mr. Drake."

Buck Weaver's slate gray eyes flicked toward the big gambler, then returned to Sarah. His undershot chin set stubbornly.

"That's just it," he said.

"What's just it?"

"I'm asking for my time."

It jarred her. Buck Weaver was as much a part of the Lazy R as the weathered house, and the corrals and the bunk shack.

She said, "Why, Buck? Why? Your job is safe. You'll continue as you always have. We won't interfere with you."

Buck Weaver shook his head slowly. He wasn't a sharp man, or a smart one. His virtue lay in dogged loyalty, in an unreasoning willingness to follow Arch Rathbone's lead, and it was that very loyalty which separated him from Sarah now.

"Your uncle didn't trust him." He didn't look at Drake, but an angry color came up beneath Drake's even windburn.

Sarah said steadily, "I know that, Buck. They didn't understand each other."

A great complaint came out of Buck Weaver. "He fought against the ranch. He sided with the Bench people."

That fact marked Drake, would always mark him in Weaver's eyes, and Sarah knew it. She said, "I asked you to fire Champion and you didn't want the job. If Drake fires him will you stay and work for us?"

An expression of crafty satisfaction flickered over Weaver's face. "If he does—"

Sarah Rathbone turned to the man she intended to marry, and her voice was slow and deliberate. "This is your chance," she said in a low voice. "In this country a man is judged by what he's done, Tom. Drive those Texans out of the valley and Cloud is yours for the asking."

Tom Drake stared at her, and from her to Weaver, and read the glowing pleasure in the man's eyes. His throat felt dry, as if the dust through which he had ridden was choking him. He understood. For some reason of her own, Sarah

125

Rathbone was putting him on trial. If he failed this test everything he'd hoped to gain would be lost. There was a lot of her uncle in this girl, a hardness that her affection for him had not softened.

"All right," he said, and marched out into the street. Darkness had come and the lamps from the store windows lighted the rutted dust like a colored checkerboard.

He moved up the sidewalk, aware that the street was deserted, knowing that a lot of people in store doorways were watching his progress.

He came to the Big Horn. He went in. The single bartender still stood behind the counter, and Champion's men still lingered about their table. Otherwise the long room was empty.

Drake hovered just inside the batwing doors, then walked to the table. He sensed the withdrawal, the suspicion of the men around Champion.

"I want to talk to you." He jerked his head toward one of the other tables. He moved away without waiting for Champion's answer and sat down with his back against the wall.

Champion took his time in following. He looked broader and squatter than usual, his thick short neck rising like a tree trunk from his unbuttoned collar.

He came over and halted, staring down at Drake, insolent and mocking. "You want to talk, huh." He kicked out a chair and planted himself on it. "What's there to talk about?"

"Trouble." Drake tried to hold his voice level, but in spite of himself he felt a slight shiver run through him. Champion was utterly inhuman. He'd known the man casually on the Kansas frontier, and he'd seemed perfect for this job. But now, with the job finished, Drake wondered if he could control the killer.

"What trouble?" Champion was watching him with a bright intentness.

"Look," Drake said, "you made a mistake when you hung the old man at the fort. His girl is a friend of Sarah Rathbone's. Sarah's given orders to get rid of you."

Champion had been drinking for most of the afternoon, but whisky appeared to have no more effect on him than water.

"Who'd she tell to get rid of me?"

"Buck Weaver."

Champion grinned hungrily. "I ain't seen him come in here to give me my time."

"He won't," Drake said. "He's afraid of you, but that isn't the point. You're putting me in a bad position."

"I'm weeping for you," Champion said.

Drake got a little desperate. "Look, Joel, I've always been your friend."

Champion dropped his right hand and patted the gun against his thigh. "This is the only friend I have, Drake. What are you getting at?"

"This," Drake said. "I managed it so that Arch Rathbone brought you up the trail, and I wrote you a letter, promising you five thousand dollars if you took my orders when you came."

"I took them."

"I haven't got the money now. I won't have it until I marry the girl and get the ranch into my name."

"And I'm staying here until you do, and then I expect to collect a lot more than five thousand."

"You'll get it." At the moment Tom Drake would have promised almost anything. "But you'll never get it if you stay here. Sarah made it plain that if I don't get rid of you, she won't marry me."

Champion shook his head. "Listen, Drake. I'm not that kind of a sucker. I go back to Texas, and that's the last I ever hear of you, or the money, or anything."

"Who mentioned Texas? Just get out of Cloud and keep out of sight. You can stay at the old fort in the hills. I don't want you to go for good until I'm sure Moffet's cleared out."

At the mention of Del Moffet's name Champion stiffened. "You think he's still in the country?"

"I think he is. I think he was on the ridge this morning when I shot up the ranch. I think he tried to follow me through the hills."

Champion pushed back his chair. "Why didn't you say so before?"

Drake blinked at him, puzzled at this reaction.

"Maybe he's getting away," Champion said. He called to his men, motioning them toward the door. Drake followed, still not understanding.

"Where you going?"

"To look for that damned Ranger." They came outside and Champion started for his horse. Drake glanced up and down the street. He saw Karen Madden appear from the marshal's office. He whistled softly, his mind working fast.

"Wait a minute," he said.

Champion had already untied his horse. "What?"

"There's the Madden girl. If anyone in the valley knows where Del Moffet is, she will. He's working for her."

Champion tied the horse again. He walked up the street, his men lounging along behind. Tom Drake stayed where he was. He wished now that he hadn't mentioned Karen. Not that he had any feeling for her, but he wanted no more trouble in Cloud this night.

Chapter Nineteen

Karen Madden saw Champion and his men moving toward her up the center of the street. Her first impulse was to duck back into the marshal's office, but she had no reason to suppose that they were coming to talk to her. She held steady until they swerved and walked directly at her, and then it was too late. She turned back toward the office, and Champion barked, "Wait."

She stopped, conscious of the sudden stir in the room behind her, aware that Boone Horn had come out onto the walk.

Champion halted less than a dozen steps away. His men fanned out into a half circle, alert and ready and watchful, old hands at this deadly game.

The marshal faced them, giving no sign that he understood. He said quietly, "Get into the office, Karen."

"No," Champion said. "I want to talk to her, old man."

"She has nothing to say to you. Go ahead, Karen."

Champion's frog eyes glazed with anger. "Grab her, Nick."

One of his men stepped forward, and Boone Horn reached for the gun at his hip. He never touched it. Champion shot him three times in the face. The heavy bullets knocked the old man backward, seeming for an instant to nail him against the wall. Then the body slid downward into a disordered heap on the boardwalk.

The action had been so swift, Karen Madden hardly realized what had happened. She started to scream, but Nick caught her by the shoulder and pulled her away from the store front.

In a sense, Nick made a mistake, for the instant he dragged Karen out of the line of fire, Lew Cashmere cut loose with the shotgun which he had snatched up from the marshal's desk.

He missed the big target. Champion, with a sixth sense for danger, had pitched himself head foremost onto the walk, but the full pattern of the shot struck the man who had been standing behind the outlaw—struck him in the stomach, almost tearing him apart.

Champion had fallen in perfect shooting position, and he emptied his gun upward, every shot catching the saloon-keeper squarely. Lew Cashmere died before his body slacked to the floor.

Two of Champion's men leaped over their prone leader and rushed the marshal's office. Belle Storm was trying to wrestle a rifle from the wall. She didn't get it down. They dragged her into the street. She fought like a cornered cat until one of them gave her a backhand slap that nearly knocked her from her feet.

She subsided then, shaking and sullen, her black eyes burning dangerously as she watched Champion rise, reload his empty gun and drop it back into its holster.

Afterward he dusted his clothes with deliberate slowness, as if to prove that the fight hadn't disturbed his nerves.

Belle glanced up and down the street. A single head appeared in one doorway, then popped back out of sight, and Champion grinned at Karen Madden.

"Well," he said, "it looks like I can talk to you now without any interruptions. Where's Moffet?"

"I don't know," Karen said.

Champion's broad hand whipped sideways, and the crack of the slap carried along the darkening street. Karen began to cry, and Champion hit her again.

"Wait, mister!" The call came from **that** doorway where Karen had seen the head appear. "**Mister,** can we come out a minute?"

Champion swiveled his head around on his thick neck, but he didn't answer.

The head showed around the door jamb, and Belle recognized Cal Mason, the freight line man. Two more heads craned cautiously around Cal's fat bulk, and Belle heard the creaking, old-man's voice that belonged to young Art Henley, one of Cal's drivers. "All we want is to come over and talk a minute," Art called, and still Champion stood there grinning.

Down the street, other heads appeared at other doors. Belle sucked in a deep breath. The townspeople might take a hand in this, after all. Some of them had courage. Some of them had guns.

She saw Cal Mason's bulk come out of the doorway. He was holding his hat in his hand and he came forward with an odd, hitching, crablike motion, like a fat boy approaching the desk of a severe teacher armed with a ruler. He said, "Listen, mister, it ain't that we want to make no trouble whatsoever, but we did think that maybe—I mean, seeing that these are girls and all, if you'd just let us take them along, we'd appreciate it. I mean, they can't do you no harm, and if we just take them out of the way—"

Joel Champion's hand came up, full of gun. The shot racketed against the false fronts. The echoes died down and Cal Mason looked at his hat. He couldn't seem to find what he was looking for and he started to raise it for a closer examination. Champion's gun bellowed again, and this time the hat flapped a little.

"Yeah," Joel Champion said. "There's two holes in it now. Get the hell back where you come from, fat man, or you'll have more holes than that."

Cal placed the hat on his head. He said, "You see how it is, Karen. I—" and then he jumped as Champion drove a bullet between his feet. He moved with astonishing speed for such a fat man. Only one more bullet hit near his flying feet, and the fifth chipped splinters off the door jamb as he disappeared.

Champion reloaded once more. He yelled, "The next town sonofabitch that sticks his head out is going to get it blowed off," and that was that. The doorways yawned

130

emptily. The town belonged to Champion and his Texas killers.

He turned around and slapped Karen Madden across the mouth.

"Leave her alone," Belle cried. "Del Moffet rode out of the country."

"Oh, did he?" Champion put his bug-eyed gaze on her. He studied her for a minute. "Who you worried about?" he asked. "Her, or that damn Ranger?"

The aptness of the question, coming from such a primitive brute, startled Belle. It showed. She knew it showed.

"Uh-huh," Champion said. "You're his girl. It figured, sister. It figured. So I'll tell you what I'm going to do. I'm going to keep the both of you under my wing, and if I know that tin star—what's the matter, girlie?"

The matter was that Belle couldn't keep the tears out of her eyes.

"If he's like he used to be," Champion said, "he'll come around to get you. That ranny was born to die noble."

He strode up the street. "Bring them along," he said over his shoulder, and one of his men shoved Belle. She stumbled, but she saw that Karen had come to the end of her strength. She put her arm around Karen's waist, steadying her, and thus, together, they were herded through the dust.

Champion reached the door of the Big Horn. He stopped and peered inside, and Tom Drake chose that time to come down the steps from the hotel. He walked out into the center of the street, and he seemed to be arguing with Champion.

Belle looked back at the men following her. She was scared, but that didn't keep her from seeking for a means of escape. If she could only slip into one of the passageways between the buildings . . . But the men were too close. She had no chance.

And then her attention focused on the hotel porch, for Sarah Rathbone had appeared there. Sarah came down the steps with Buck Weaver in her wake, and she marched into the street with all the arrogance Arch could have asked for.

Suddenly Belle began to hurry Karen. She wanted to be close when Sarah faced Champion. She made it in time to hear Sarah say in a furious voice, "You're through in this valley. Get your men and ride out."

Champion laughed in sheer amusement. "You're the

131

one," he said, and there was a note of respect in his tone. "Aren't you afraid of anything?"

"Why should I be?"

He might have pointed out to her that two men lay dead behind him, and that his crew controlled Cloud completely. He didn't bother.

He said, "I'm not riding. I like it here. I'll stay, and I'll run this country any way I want."

Sarah looked to Tom Drake. He looked elsewhere.

"I might even marry you some time," Champion said, and chuckled at his joke. "You'd be a match for a man."

She stared at him hard. Then without a word she turned on her heel and strode back toward the hotel. The movement caught Buck Weaver unprepared. He found himself alone, facing the outlaw.

Champion said, "Want a part of this, Buck?"

Weaver struggled with himself. Every instinct, every ounce of his training, told him to draw. And yet it would be suicide to draw against this Texas crew. He held his hands wide, away from his hips, and the gesture said louder than any words that he was through.

Champion waited a while to let Weaver taste the gall of his surrender. Then he said, "Haul your gun out slow and drop it in the dust."

Buck Weaver obeyed. Champion stepped in and swiped his gun barrel across the foreman's face, breaking the skin, bringing blood, knocking Weaver to his knees.

"That's to show you who the boss is." He jabbed Weaver in the ribs with his gun muzzle. "All right. On your feet."

Weaver managed to drag himself upright.

"Get your horse and ride out. If I ever see you again I'll kill you."

Weaver shambled unsteadily toward his horse. As he did so he heard Drake snarl at Champion, "You fool. You've ruined me with the girl. She'll never marry me now, never."

Champion laughed heartily. "You don't know how to handle women. Come on, I'll show you. When I'm finished with her she'll be glad to marry anybody."

Weaver rode out, the rasp of the outlaw's laughter grating his ears. He pounded across the bridge and drove up the winding grade, swaying slightly in the saddle. His head felt split open. Blood oozed from the gash across his forehead. He didn't see the other horseman pull out of the brush along the trail.

"Pull up," the rider said.

Weaver pulled up, too startled to react any other way. Then he recognized Del Moffet and his hand dropped automatically toward the empty holster at his hip.

Moffet saw the gesture in the moonlight and one of his own guns blossomed in his hand. "Hold it, Weaver."

Buck Weaver's shoulders sagged. That instinctive grab for his missing gun represented the last spasm of his shattered courage. In one day he had seen his whole world collapse. In one day he, the second most powerful man in the valley, had become a beaten fugitive, running for his life.

"All right," he said. "All right. You killed Arch, but Champion will get you."

"I didn't kill Arch."

Something in the way Moffet said it jolted Buck Weaver's conviction. An hour ago he would have sneered at the statement. Now he said, "You didn't?"

"Champion shot him from the yard. Tom Drake was up on the rim, throwing lead at the bunkhouse."

"The dirty bastard," Weaver said.

It took no effort at all to believe Moffet. Weaver knew all he needed to know about Champion, and he already hated Drake.

"What happened in town?" Moffet asked.

Weaver told him. "Champion's in control of the place," he said. "The man isn't human, and he and his riders are drunk. With Boone Horn and Cashmere dead there isn't a man to stand against them." He sat his horse somberly, but then he brightened, some of his old spirit returning. "My crew's out in the hills—still hunting you probably, but they'll drift back to the ranch. We can pick them up by morning—"

"And what happens to those women in the meantime?"

"I don't know!" The words burst out of Weaver. "The man's an animal, he's worse than an animal."

Moffet swung his horse around. Weaver said tensely in a high voice, "What do you think you're going to do?"

"Get Champion. I should have done it before."

"You haven't a chance. They'll be watching this trail, thinking some of the crew might ride in, thinking I might come back." The thought flashed through his mind that ten minutes ago he had felt nothing but hate for Moffet, and now he was worrying about what would happen when he rode into Cloud.

"Is there another way into town?"

Weaver chewed pensively at his lower lip. "We can get across the creek a mile above here and work down the canyon and come in across the meadow behind the livery."

"Show me."

Buck Weaver led the way. They forded the stream, worked over the rough ground, and finally came back across the looping Crazy Woman.

The irregular row of Cloud's buildings made their dark patch against the night sky. Weaver said, "I never thought I'd be riding with you, Moffet."

Del Moffet didn't answer. His mind was on the town, on what Champion and his drunken riders might do to the three girls. Somehow he had to stop Champion, and there was only one way to do it. But Champion had six riders with him. No, five. Weaver had told him how Cashmere had shotgunned the sixth man.

Five riders, and Champion, and Drake. Seven men in all. If he could catch them bunched . . . But that was too much to expect, and he'd get no help from anybody in Cloud, either. Boone Horn and Cashmere were dead, and he'd long since taken the measure of the town's ordinary citizens.

He had Weaver, but Weaver needed a gun. He'd just have to feel his way from here on out, hoping his chance would come.

They rode across the last stretch of meadow, the thick carpet of grass deadening the sound of their horses' feet. They entered the dusty alley which ran behind the livery barn, and turned into the runway to dismount.

A man had been standing at the front door, gaping up the street. His mouth broke apart with surprise as he saw them.

Moffet said, "Come here, Nosy."

Nosy Perkins sidled toward them. He said, "What are you all doing here?"

"Never mind that. Where's Champion and his men?"

The barn man licked his lips. "Down at the hotel. They herded those women in the lobby and—"

"Got a gun?"

134

Nosy sputtered. "Now wait a minute. I ain't no fighter. I'm—"

"For Buck Weaver."

Nosy's relief took the form of a loud sigh. "There's a shotgun in the office."

"Get it, and all the shells you have."

Nosy trotted away. He came back eagerly, carrying the gun in one hand, the box of shells in the other. Weaver took the box, examined the shells and said in a disgusted voice, "Bird shot."

"All right," Moffet said. "It'll make a noise."

Weaver stared at him, not understanding. He said, "We've got to get them out of that hotel. We can't have them forting up there, using the women as a shield."

"Oh," Weaver said.

"I'm going down the alley behind the hotel," Moffet went on. "I could crash in there, but one of the women might get hurt. I want to get below the Big Horn."

Buck Weaver nodded. His eyes began to glow.

"Give me five minutes, then step out into the street and cut loose with the shotgun. Keep firing as long as you can after they come out of the hotel. I want them headed this way before they realize I'm in town."

"All right."

"And have your horse ready in case they get too close to you. Bird shot is poor stuff to go up against a forty-five with."

"You'll get yourself killed," Weaver objected.

"Maybe, maybe not. It's a chance I've got to take. The minute I start shooting they're going to turn back on me. When they do, you make a dash for the marshal's office. There must be guns there somewhere. Get one, and we'll have Champion's crowd between us."

Leaving Weaver to digest that, he strode toward the rear of the barn. Nosy Perkins came after him. Moffet stopped. "Where do you think you're going, Nosy?"

"I'm going to get up on Thompson's store roof," Nosy said. "I'm going to see this. It'll give me something to talk about for the rest of my life."

Moffet grunted and went on. He glided along the alley's shadowed length, slipped behind the marshal's office, behind the hotel, then cut toward the street between Cloud's store and the furniture establishment.

135

He halted at the edge of the boardwalk, trying to steady his uneven breathing, trying to imagine what would be going on within the hotel.

And then, far up the street a figure stepped from the wide doorway of the livery and stood in the path of yellow light flowing from Nosy Perkins' office lantern.

A shotgun blast broke the night, echoing with rebounding clatter through the town. Another blast followed as Buck Weaver let go with the second barrel.

There was an interval of pulsing silence. Moffet knew Weaver must be reloading. And then men burst across the hotel porch and spilled down the steps.

The first man had barely reached the edge of the sidewalk when Weaver fired his third blast, calling full attention upon himself.

The men ducked right and left, taking advantage of the building shadows, calling back and forth across the roadway, their voices high with excitement yet thick with drink.

They were moving away from Moffet, all their concentration on the single figure before the livery. Buck Weaver stood firm, making a target of himself, and Moffet had a moment's admiration for the man. Weaver wasn't fighting for himself, or even for Sarah. He was fighting for the Lazy R. To old hands like Weaver the ranch was everything. It commanded a loyalty closely akin to patriotism.

And then Moffet moved along the walk. He'd seen what he'd been waiting for. Joel Champion had appeared on the hotel gallery.

Squat and square and solid, Champion peered up the street. Then he came casually down the steps, calling as he came, "Who is it? What's the shooting?"

Someone shouted from across the street, "Looks like that fool foreman you ran out of town. Must have gone loco—" and two fresh blasts from Buck Weaver's borrowed gun cut off the last words.

Champion jumped the remaining step to the sidewalk. Moffet said, "This way, Joel. Look this way," and stepped sidewise into the ribbon of dust.

Champion swung about, his high, hoarse shout riding up through the night. "Moffet!"

"Come on," Moffet said, his voice carrying in the sudden silence. "Come on, Joel. You've been waiting for the chance to kill me. Here it is, man."

136

He stood tense, expecting Champion's gun to swing up. A good two hundred yards separated them. He wished he were closer. He wanted no misses, no delays. But Champion fooled him. Instead of walking toward Moffet, the outlaw leaped sidewise for the passage which ran back toward the alley between the hotel and the next building.

Del sent two shots after him, one striking the corner of the hotel just at Champion's right, the other striking the window of the store beyond.

Champion was gone, and in return bullets hammered at Del from further up the street. He jumped back across the sidewalk and into a passageway beside Seth Cloud's store.

He paused, breathing heavily, cursing under his breath. He'd tried to draw Champion out of the hotel, away from the women, and he'd failed. Champion would run around the building and in through the rear door.

And the surprise had fizzled out. The men up the street knew he was here and would be hunting him. They'd lost all interest in Buck Weaver.

Champion would be covering the alley, waiting for him to come out that way, while the others rushed along the street to cut him off from behind. He glanced upward. He had nowhere to go but up.

This building was made of logs, its roof a slanting flatness covered with sod, the roof timbers pole pine, cut long, thrust out to make an overhang a good foot beyond the building wall.

He slipped the guns back into their holsters. He jumped up and caught one of the rafters with both hands, finding a chink between the logs for a toehold.

The next second, he flopped belly flat upon the sod of the roof, swinging his legs up in the same motion. He lay quiet for a while, and then, knowing that if they failed to find him on the ground they'd be bound to think of searching the roofs, he came up to his hands and knees and crawled the width of the building.

Down below, the street and alleys gave forth muffled shouts as Champion's men combed the town for him. The roars of the shotgun had ceased. He wondered what had happened to Buck Weaver, then forgot the foreman.

A five foot passageway ran between the building on which he squatted and its next-door neighbor. He peered down into it, saw nothing in the shadows, and rose slowly to his feet. He backed up four steps, took a running jump and landed with a thud on the shakes of the adjoining roof.

To his straining ears, the thump sounded loud enough to be heard all over town. He crouched on the slanting surface, listening, waiting for an outcry of discovery.

None came. He crawled over the ridge of the roof and down its far side. The wall of the hotel faced him, its row of darkened windows looking like empty eyes. He had time to feel thankful that nobody had lighted a lamp that might cast its glow out across the roof, and then he slid to the wooden gutter which bordered the roof's edge.

There he stopped, sitting on the rough shakes, his feet braced against the gutter. The hotel wall was some three feet distant, a window directly above him.

He stood up, leaning forward gingerly until he could get one hand on the window sill, reaching outward with the other to test the sash. It was locked.

Moffet whistled silently through his teeth, his habitual expression of disappointment. He studied the frame, wondering if he could jiggle the catch loose without breaking the glass, but the fit seemed too solid.

He drew his left hand gun and tapped gently at the glass just over the catch. He increased the tapping, praying that he wouldn't shatter the whole pane, and for once his luck held. A half-moon crack appeared, about twice the size of a silver dollar.

He got out his knife, The putty was rotten, all its oil dried out by the sun, he dug it out and the half-moon fell, striking the hard ground below with a tiny tinkle.

He inserted one finger, pushed the catch aside and raised the sash. A moment later he lowered himself into the room. He listened, hearing no sound but his own hoarse breathing.

He tiptoed across the room, striking a corner of the washstand in the darkness, and eased the hall door open as quietly as he could.

The hinges squeaked as the door swung inward, admitting yellow light from the hall. Again he froze, his hand on his gun.

He heard the murmur of voices from a room across the hall, women's voices. Softly he stepped out into the light and put an ear against the opposite panel. He recognized Sarah Rathbone's deep contralto and Belle's lighter tones, and knew a quick, heartening upsurge of relief. For the moment, at least, they were all right.

He glided to the stairs and peered down their straight well at the lobby below. It seemed to be deserted. He took the steps cautiously, making no sound but painfully aware that anyone who might look through the front windows could see him.

But he gained the ground floor without incident. He crossed to the dining room door, easing it inward. The room beyond was inky dark.

He slid through the crack, pushed the door gently closed behind him and started to move toward the kitchen. He had taken only one step when the swinging gun slashed down, nearly tearing off his ear and striking the point of his shoulder with paralyzing force.

His own gun slipped from his nerveless fingers and fell to the uncarpeted boards with a dull clatter.

Instinct brought him around, raising his right arm to protect his head. The unseen man swung again and his heavy, bony wrist chopped against this arm. Moffet could feel the hot breath on his face, and hear the grunt as the attacker's forearm struck his own.

He crouched, letting his knees buckle. He reached out with both hands to catch the man's waist. Then he straightened suddenly, pushing with all the force of his leg muscles, and lifted the man clear of the floor to struggle in his locked arms. They fell together across the long dining table. Their combined weight snapped its stringer supports and it collapsed with a crash, spilling dishes and cutlery in a jumbled mass.

The man under Moffet cursed in a monotonous undertone as he struggled to free himself. Somehow his efforts seemed panicky, as if he lacked the stomach for this fight and was trying harder to get away than to cripple his opponent.

Suddenly he yelled, crying out Champion's name in the darkness, and for the first time Moffet realized that he had tangled with Tom Drake.

Feet pounded across the kitchen. The connecting door whipped open, letting in a wide band of yellow light. And then Joel Champion's bulky form blocked out part of the light.

The outlaw stopped in the doorway, blinking, trying to

see in the yellow-mottled darkness of the dining room, trying to decide which of the big struggling bodies belonged to Moffet. And in that instant Moffet broke free and rolled backward, cutting his hand on a sharp wedge of broken plate.

He caught up the plate, hurling it into Champion's face. As its jagged corner struck Champion's cheek he stumbled back a step and his gun exploded. The bullet buried itself in the wall at Moffet's side.

Moffet rolled over and came to his feet. He saw the dining room window. He went through it, taking the glass with him, protecting his face with his folded arms. He landed on his back on the hard earth. It drove most of the breath out of him, but he rolled and came upright, and half groped, half scrambled along the passage to the alley.

A gun roared behind him as he rounded the corner. He reached down and found his right hand gun still in its holster. He lifted it, peering back, and saw someone lean from the dining room window.

He fired, and Tom Drake pitched head first into the narrow passage.

Shouts boiled up from the street. He swung away, saw Champion appear at the hotel's rear door, and drove the outlaw to cover with a shot which thudded into the door frame an inch from Champion's head.

But what move could he make next? He was trapped. He couldn't stay in the alley without drawing fire from Champion, lurking in the kitchen doorway, and he couldn't run the length of the passageway to the street, for Champion's men were there. Suddenly he thought of the dining room window. They wouldn't expect him to use it; he'd just dived out of it. He darted back toward the window.

Tom Drake lay against the hotel wall, light in an upper window reflecting from the neighboring building and shining dully upon his face.

Moffet hardly glanced at him. He and Drake had knocked out all the glass from the frame, diving out, so he had no trouble swinging up and into the litter of the dining room.

The door to the kitchen was still open and the path of light showed him the wreckage of the crumpled table and the broken dishes. He skirted around it, came to the door jamb and looked beyond.

Champion was at the alley entrance, twenty feet from him, his back to the dining room as he stared out into the night. Moffet took a silent step into the room, his face grim, his clothes torn and bloody.

"You're looking the wrong way, Joel."

Champion's broad back hunched convulsively. He threw himself sidewise, twisting to face Moffet, and the gun in his big hand blasted as he spun. One bullet lifted a splinter from the floor between Moffet's feet. Another struck the jamb beside Moffet's hip.

Moffet took his time. He shot Joel Champion between the eyes.

Chapter Twenty

The gunfire from the hotel seemed to fill the town, but despite his vantage point on the roof Nosy Perkins couldn't see what was going on.

Buck Weaver had emptied his shotgun a last time and dropped it in the dust. He'd run through the livery to the alley and along the alley to the rear of the marshal's office. He'd hardly reached it when the shooting started in the hotel.

All this was too much for Nosy Perkins. He reared up, yelling down at Weaver, "They're in the hotel. Hear them? They're in the hotel." He stood outlined against the lighter sky and one of Champion's men across the street saw him. The Texan lifted his gun and shot Nosy off the roof.

Buck Weaver's frantic search had disclosed a gun in Boone Horn's desk. He whirled and ran to the open door, just in time to catch the flash of the gun which killed Nosy. He fired. A yell came from the shadows. The Texan took two running steps before he collapsed in the dust.

Champion's four remaining riders had been closing in on

the hotel. They turned at the sound of the shots and started to sprint toward the marshal's office. Weaver got the first one. The other three ducked back, only to have Moffet's gun open up on them from the lobby door.

Suddenly the fight went out of them. From the shadows into which they dived, a shaken cry rose through the night.

"Moffet—Moffet!"

"Yeah?" He held his fire, waiting in the darkness beside one of the porch pillars.

"Where's Champion?"

"Dead."

"We quit."

"All right. Drop your guns and come out into the middle of the street, hands high."

They obeyed.

"Weaver?"

Buck Weaver stepped out of the marshal's office. He paused beside the twisted body of Nosy Perkins, muttering, then came up behind the prisoners.

"Take their guns and let them ride," Moffet said.

After searching the pair, Weaver marched them to their horses. As they rode out of town he said in a disappointed voice, "If my crew was here I'd hang the lot."

"There's been enough killing," Moffet said. "Champion's dead in the kitchen, Tom Drake outside the dining room window."

Buck Weaver looked him over, noting his cut hand, the lacerated arm, the torn clothes. "Where's the women?" he asked.

"Locked in a room upstairs. Get them."

Moffet walked away utterly weary. He found a chair beside the lobby desk and sank into it.

They came down, Sarah leading, Karen and Belle following her, Al Chase and his white-faced wife bringing up the rear.

Sarah Rathbone had a bruise on her cheek and her dress was torn. Moffet grinned with wicked pleasure. She'd been pushed around, and if ever a woman deserved it she did. Then he heaved himself out of the chair and went to Belle.

"You all right?"

She nodded, wincing at sight of the blood which oozed from the arm he had cut as he went through the window.

142

Sarah Rathbone said, "Weaver says you killed both Champion and Drake."

He didn't even bother to look at her.

She took a deep breath, and the words came with difficulty. "He also says Champion killed Arch on Tom's orders. I have to believe him. Unless Tom had contact with Champion he couldn't have known they'd hung Pete. I made a big mistake in Drake, but I hope you don't think I had any part in Arch's death."

He turned then, saying tiredly, "What difference does it make what I think?"

She took a long time to answer. "I—things are a lot changed with Arch gone. You thought he owed you something, that he stole money from your family."

Moffet shrugged.

"I'll make you a deal," she said, forthright as a man. "I need someone to run the ranch. After what's happened I don't want to stay in the valley."

"Sorry," Moffet said, but she didn't seem to hear him. She was a Rathbone, arrogant still.

"I need someone strong," she went on. "I've made up my mind in the last hour. I'm going to take Belle and go East."

Moffet looked at Belle, standing silent, watching him, her dark eyes very large in her white face. Sarah Rathbone had money. Sarah could give Belle many things, but she would demand much in return. She was taking Belle, not for the girl's own good, but as a defense against her own loneliness.

He said gently, "Texas or the East?"

Sarah didn't understand but Belle did. Her lips formed the word, "Texas."

Moffet forgot his aching arm, his bruised body, his weariness.

"Let Weaver run the ranch," he told Sarah. "Tear up those quit-claim deeds to the north Bench and let Karen Madden bring the people back."

"That part's all right, but I'd rather you—"

"Look," he said. "All your life you've grabbed what you wanted, hurting other people. Tonight you got hurt, and now you want somebody to hold on to, somebody you can dictate to. If that's the way it has to be for a Rathbone, all right. But find yourself somebody new, lady. Belle

143

has things of her own to do. Belle has a trip of her own to take."

He took Belle by the hand and walked toward the door. "A trip with me," he said over his shoulder. "A trip for keeps, to Texas."